# SILVER FOX GRUMP

EVIE ROSE

Copyright © 2025 by Evie Rose

All rights reserved.

No part of this book may be reproduced in any form or by any electronic or mechanical means, including information storage and retrieval systems, without written permission from the author, except for the use of brief quotations in a book review.

This story is a work of fiction. Names, characters, places, and incidents are the product of the author's imagination or are used fictitiously. Any resemblance to actual events, locales, or persons, living or dead, is coincidental.

Cover: © 2025 by Evie Rose. Images under licence from Deposit Photos.

1
---
SEV

Poking the dead body of the Battersea double-agent with my toe, I hope it'll help. I used to get a buzz out of this sort of thing.

I wait.

Nope. Nothing.

I am just not as bloodthirsty as I was.

Perhaps turning thirty-nine stole all the joy out of life. I'm so old.

"Clean up," I direct my second-in-command and stride out of the basement interrogation room—it's whimsically called the executive exercise suite—and shove my hands in my pockets. I'm tempted by the stairs, but there are twenty floors in this building and that's enough for even me to break into a sweat.

How is it possible for a mafia boss to be bored? I punch the button to call the elevator.

Making obscene amounts of money? Most people's idea of a good time.

Being respected and revered? I believe people aspire to this.

Death. That's supposed to be exciting, or at least distressing, but I find it rather dull now.

I even have family and friends. One of my triplet brothers lives here in London, and I've been thinking about how to drag the other back from Milan to have the three of us together, and Wes Matthews, the kingpin of Mitcham, counts as a friend.

Avoiding my own gaze in the mirrored little box, I consider going to the penthouse to pretend to relax.

But I cannot shake the feeling of loneliness, and being at the top of a tower won't help that.

I need a fucking hobby.

Or perhaps just to reconnect with the legit part of my business? Maybe that will provide a challenge of some sort. On impulse, I punch the ground floor button. When the elevator slides to a halt, I prowl out.

The huge entrance hall is empty, as it should be, just a receptionist at his post, a security guard, and that idiot stray cat, who trots up to me like we're best friends. But it's not tranquil. There's the sound of laughter and chat coming from one of the main conference rooms, and I narrow my eyes as I reach down to scratch between the ears of the ginger tom cat who has adopted Morden Company as his home. What's going on?

My feet thud on the marble floor as I stride towards the noise, leaving the cat behind.

Throwing open the double doors, my jaw clenches as the room falls silent.

"What the fuck is going on here?" I say into the horrified hush.

There are balloons. In Morden Company. We build skyscrapers and bury bodies.

Fucking *balloons*.

One man is mid-way through a dance move that he borrowed from the seventies, a woman has a microphone, another is holding a potted *plant*, and there's music playing. There are snacks on tables.

"Mr Blackwood." A woman I recognise as the head of HR and the bane of my life hustles up to me. She's in her fifties and wearing a sensible navy dress. "This is the welcome and getting-to-know-you party for the new recruits."

A welcome party? They get *salaries*. What do they need a party for?

"Who signed off on this?" I snarl.

"I believe that was you, sir."

"No, I told you to stop hiring idiots who quit." There is a dead man in the basement, but here my staff are hanging out like it's a school disco for eleven-year-olds.

"That's right, Mr Blackwood. These are the best and brightest!"

"Really?" I glance around the room. Half of them are wearing T-shirts. "Oh fuck."

A tickle of recollection comes to me. Florence begged me to do something about the high turnover of staff at Morden.

"But there was a…" She coughs awkwardly. "Slight issue with retention of the younger personnel that you ordered us to employ to grow Morden Company's online presence. We tracked it down to workplace comfort expectations of Gen Z, compared to previous generations. Due to technological changes and economic uncertainty, they have different values."

"Values," I mutter under my breath.

"This welcome event has reduced the need for new hiring by twenty per cent." Florence preens slightly. She has the confidence of a Morden employee who has survived years in my company and knows I respect hard work and results above all. "This provides a chance for our newest staff to bond so they feel like valued members of the team."

Sounds like the kind of thing I agreed to when I was feeling tired of the mafia aspect of my business and imagined if I threw myself into the legitimate part I'd feel magically better.

My lip curls.

Wonderful. If this attempt to fix my mood is a failure too, I'm left with nothing but phoning one of my brothers or Wes, and drinking copious amounts of whisky.

"What do you think?" I ask, turning to the terrified audience. "Does this help you feel like a 'valued member of the team'?" I don't bother to keep the cynicism from my tone.

The cotton-clad children stare at the floor.

I roll my eyes. "Relax. I won't throw you into the dungeon for talking in my presence."

Someone titters.

That wasn't a joke, and I remain stone-faced. They're all aware I'm a mafia boss, as well as the CEO of this company that fronts up Morden's darker activities. You'd have to have been hiding under a rock the size of Manchester to not know.

"I mainly kill people for being stupid, and presumably you all have bits of paper saying you have qualifications," I drawl. Unlike me. I have scars to prove my suitability for the job of Morden kingpin. "So you can't be totally brainless. So speak up."

"That's not reassuring," someone mutters, almost inaudibly.

"I'm your boss, not your therapist," I snap back.

Behind me, there's a gentle sound of pain.

Florence. Right, yes. This was supposed to increase staff retention by showing we value them as individuals and I'm a reasonable employer. Well, one out of two isn't bad.

This was a mistake. I am not a good boss, I am a cantankerous, sarcastic, scarred arsehole and I should let these young people—I will concede they aren't children, just— alone to enjoy their party and be effective members of staff when they're done.

"Glad to see morale is high." I spin on my heel and chatter starts up as I head to the door.

It must be a voice that makes me stop and look around.

At the side of the group, previously hidden by a tall man, there's a girl. Quite an unassuming little thing, with short black hair and a smile that's like looking into the sun in June as she offers the person next to her a cupcake from a clear plastic tub.

She has sparkling brown eyes. She's tiny, barely tall enough to reach my shoulder. She's wearing dangly earrings, a blue skirt that is utterly flick-up-able, and a white blouse. There's a subtle gold necklace around her neck, and no rings on her left hand.

My heart lurches as a middle-aged man takes a palepink iced cupcake from her stash. It has swirls of buttercream. I glower as he bites into it, anger and jealousy burning in my throat.

*That* is for me.

I'm across the room and in front of her in a second. She blinks up into my face.

"What are those?" I ask abruptly.

I mean to have a bit more tact and open my mouth to say something more, but then she turns her unexpected weapon on me.

Fuck, her smile. It's the most beautiful thing I've ever seen. She's like I've been living in black and white, and suddenly there's colour.

I stare at her.

I'd never realised until now how brave it is to smile. How being happy and positive is leaving yourself so totally vulnerable. I'm probably twice her age and three times her size, and I don't let people in by smiling like that.

She's just standing in front of a man who scared and threatened everyone in this room, and instead of bowing her head or looking as nervous as she should be, she's *smiling*. As though it's easy.

I admire it.

"Cupcakes." Her voice is high but lyrical. "Would you like one?"

I am not a cupcake sort of person. I am not a person for sweet treats. I like whisky that tastes like burnt Scottish soil having a reunion in a morgue.

Apparently, now, I like *her*.

It's not that she's young and beautiful, although that definitely helps. It's that I'm suddenly achingly aware that taking care of this girl would fill a need I had no idea about. A gap in my chest that I hadn't even recognised was in the space that I always assumed had my withered, charred excuse for a heart.

I don't know how to love her as she deserves. I haven't a clue how to make her love me. Both those things feel very important, and I can't believe I've neglected them as skills.

There's a pause while I'm flummoxed by unfamiliar

feelings, and I'm still scowling. Which is maybe why a young guy pushes in from the side.

"This is Mr Blackwood." He pronounces my name like it's "God". "He doesn't want your pathetic little cakes." He's barely more than a boy, and wears a shiny suit that likely cost him more than he can afford.

She jolts like he's smacked her, and her smile falters.

"Of course not. I didn't think he would." She begins to pull away, her expression going from sunny to hurt in a second.

I'm so busy looking at her, I don't anticipate the disaster.

The man's elbow connects with the girl's, and her tub upends. Instantly, the cakes topple out, smacking onto the floor and rolling off, leaving smears of pink icing.

She watches in horror, and the man laughs.

Anger flares through me.

"Oh!" She sounds like she might cry and goes to fall to her knees.

"No." My hand shoots out. I grab her wrist where she's holding the plastic tub, then just as quickly let it go. But that split second of contact tingles. Soft. So soft and breakable. "Leave it. I want..."

I thankfully manage to not say more. *You. Everything. Your sweet pink pussy that I bet tastes even better than anything you have there.*

She's mine.

Instead, I just take the remaining cupcake from the tub and bring it to my lips. She watches, and my cock responds, thickening in my boxers as the paper case peels from the cake. It's borderline erotic, as though I'm removing that prissy little blouse from her warm skin.

It feels good. Really good. I can't remember the last time I got turned on from nothing. I feel *alive*.

I take a bite of the cupcake, and flavour and texture explode in my mouth. Sweet, soft butter icing, moist, crumbly smooth vanilla cake that melts and a flare of sharp raspberry sauce. It's the best thing I've ever tasted, and I'm floored.

Shocked.

Devastated. Where has this been my whole life? And I don't think it's actually the cake. I think it's *her*. I regard the girl, with her straight black hair, so innocent and yet... I want her.

I *need* her.

"How is it?" she ventures, smiling again.

"Very..." I stop. Orgasmic is an inappropriate reply. "Nice", or "tasty" is utterly inadequate. I opt for, "Sweet."

It's the wrong thing to say, as although she nods in agreement, her eyes lose that spark. Fuck. Should have said, "orgasmic".

I'll destroy her enemies in lieu of being eloquent.

"Is that how you treat your colleagues?" I turn to the man who tried to embarrass my girl. "Call their work pathetic? Scare them so they drop things?"

I take another bite of her heavenly cupcake. Still, I bet it's not as good as her pussy.

"I was trying to save you, sir. As you say, it's too sweet, and this whole thing is ridiculous. I'm here to work for you, not to engage in some social club." The young man has a smooth, square jaw and straight nose he's probably proud of. As though he had anything to do with his face being pretty, and not having fought for everything he owns makes him a special, chosen one somehow. I have no time for that sort of arrogance. I built and stole and clawed my way to where I am now, and genetics had nothing to do with it.

"You doubt my capacity to protect myself from a

cupcake?" I say, a little louder, finishing the cake in two more efficient bites, and screwing up the paper. I will ensure everyone understands this lesson.

"No! You slay cupcakes, sir. I merely sought to save you the inconvenience..." He trails off. His gaze is fixed suddenly on my hands, so I reach out and drop the paper case before him. It bounces at his feet, with the rest of the ruined cupcakes.

He gulps, eyes not shifting from my wrists. He can't see my tattoos, they begin in snaking patterns over my forearms. But he's freaked out. It starts to dawn on the boy that he may have made a mistake. I see the realisation rising up his face like bile from his stomach.

"Pick it up. And the cakes, too."

I barely watch as he prostrates himself, because the girl has followed the line of his eyes and is also looking at my wrists. She's gone pale.

And then I notice. There's a fine spray of red over my white cuff and dove-grey suit sleeve. No one could imagine that it's my blood, and it's not a smear, or a speck. This is the sort of pattern of blood that is created by an instrument of torture.

Damnit. Should have accepted the rubber gloves my second-in-command offered. But it *just doesn't feel the same*. And honestly, threats are better received from a guy in a suit, than one looking as though he's about to wash dishes.

"Say sorry to her." I nod at the girl as the man clambers back to his feet, the paper wrapper and wrecked cupcakes in his hands.

His pause tells me everything I need to know. He's a dick.

"I apologise if you took offence." He fails to look her in the eyes.

Can't say I didn't give him a chance, but if he can't repeat "sorry", he has no place in Morden.

"Florence, is Charlie done in the executive exercise suite?" I refer to my second-in-command.

"I believe not, Mr Blackwood," comes the reply after a moment.

"Your lucky day." He just avoided being murdered immediately by me not wanting to overload my staff with work. "Florence, as you know, runs the HR department. Since you don't have the right instincts for working in this team, she will help you with the paperwork to leave Morden Company."

"But—" the boy splutters.

"I might think Florence is full to the brim with the smelliest of shit when it comes to what's needed to retain staff, but she's better at this particular brand of bullshit than I am, and that's why I employ her. But if you disrespect her," I point at the short, black-haired girl who is watching this exchange open-mouthed, "you disrespect me."

"Sir, you have to understand—" His backtracking is tedious, and intended to save his life.

"Don't worry, you'll have a generous pay-off." My lips tighten into a thin line. "I suggest you use it to go on a trip somewhere far away and consider your choices."

Florence takes a sharp intake of breath.

There's a simple code in Morden. I have an excellent assassin—a woman in her forties who looks like someone's bumbling mother—who disposes of anyone, anywhere in the world. Zoe loves nothing more than travelling for work. Apparently, she has a social media travel channel. Perfect cover. And if an employee leaves Morden and moves abroad, they're never heard of again.

"You," I glance back to the girl. "Come with me."

I indicate the exit and practically herd her out of the room like I'm a bad, bad sheepdog who has just discovered a succulent, lonely lamb.

We don't speak on the way up to my private office. It's all I can do to not grab her. Scare her.

I'm not a caring pet dog, I'm a wolf, intent on consuming her. The only question is how best to do it.

Closing the door behind us, I sink into my office chair and regard my vulnerable little prey. She has followed obediently, and now stands before my desk, still clutching her empty cupcake tub, and looking the exact combination of confused but brave that is the recipe to undo me.

She's young. Big eyes.

I consider some options: I could order her to lean over the desk and fuck her senseless. It's a good one, and I like it, but it has the slight disadvantage of meaning I'll have to kill at least some of the HR department when they object. And I'll already be on thin ice from telling Florence to give a generous end-of-employment package to that prick so I can have him murdered for being awful.

The next option is to try a longer game. Keep her close and see if I can lure her in.

"What were you employed to do?" I ask.

"I'm a junior administrative assistant," she says tentatively.

Oh good, I definitely have things she can assist with. Administering to my every need, for instance. This is going to work out well.

"You'll be assisting me." I have a perfectly adequate PA already, but fine. I'm a mafia boss, which is basically like being a very privileged and homicidal toddler. I require a lot of assistance.

"Yes, Mr. Blackwood." She drags her gaze over my face, and I like to think that bright smile is all for me.

My desk phone shrills, and I mentally curse.

*Wes Matthews, Incoming Call.*

*7 Missed Calls.*

What?

# 2
## SEV

"Don't move," I tell my potential wife. Yes. That feels right. My wife-to-be, she just doesn't know it yet.

"Wes," I answer with what I hope is a clip that implies "Make this quick, I have a beautiful and completely inappropriate woman to claim".

"Have you got my daughter?"

I stare at the girl as all the blood drains from me. "Your daughter?"

The girl's eyes go wide.

"She's run away. Disappeared." Wes sounds stressed. "And there's something in her search history suggesting she applied for a job with you."

"I don't make hiring decisions for the legal stuff," I reply truthfully.

She shakes her head quickly, and mouths, "Please." Her big brown eyes look into mine, and beg.

This is not the sort of begging I was thinking of.

"I don't know anything about it." Denial. Totally healthy, right?

Wes makes a frustrated noise. "Could you not be an arsehole, for once in your life, and check?"

Bouncing my gaze between my best friend's daughter and my computer screen, my brows knitted with irritation, I pull up employment records.

"Miss Maisie Matthews," I say after a moment. "Twenty-one years old."

I have tattoos older than this girl. I was doing terrible things when she was innocently learning to toddle around on baby legs.

She presses her pink lips together. Black hair, brown eyes. I can see the shadow of my best friend's features in her face now. Except Wes is a six-foot-seven chiselled piece of granite, and his daughter is delicate and sweet as a doll. She looks like I could lift her with one hand.

"Good." He lets out a huff. "Keep her safe until my men can pick her up, will you?"

"You don't want her working?" I ask neutrally, watching Maisie.

"You're kidding me? No," Wes snaps. "No, she's a mafia princess. She's a child. She doesn't work in an office. Especially not in Morden Company."

Maisie's eyes fill with panic, and she presses her palms together in prayer, to me. Her god in this situation. Her dad's best friend, and she's hoping I'll save her.

There's a knife edge of decision.

For a second I teeter, wondering if my loyalty to my old friend comes first.

"There is a problem with that, though," I say carefully. "She's already my employee."

Maisie has re-oriented everything around her, like she's the sun and I've been living underground. She is my only priority now.

"Sack her."

"I can't dismiss her over nothing, Wes. That's not how we do things." We will do anything, Wes and I, but it needs a justification.

"She's my daughter!" he explodes.

I hold her gaze. "If she fancies playing at being an office bunny for a while, it would be fine, wouldn't it?"

Hurt and hope flow over Maisie's expression in equal measure.

Wes swears colourfully, and I wait for his anger to burn out. He'll realise I'm right before long.

"No, no. Absolutely not," he concludes. "I'll send over a car, and pay you for the inconvenience of losing your new staff member."

"Or you can let her work for me." My heart hammers in my chest. "I promise to look after her. What else is she good for?"

Definitely hurt this time, but she rallies, keeping her chin up, and fighting back her emotions with an expression that combines ingratiating cheerfulness with begging.

"She's my *daughter*, Sev, you'll understand when you have one."

"I doubt that." I mean the daughter as much as the attitude. I've just met the only woman I'll ever want children with, and that door has slammed shut in my face. She's forbidden.

"You're not going to keep her locked up all day making cupcakes when she has..." I reel off her qualifications from the file. I don't know if they're good or not, but she was smart enough to get employed at Morden Company, so they're not shabby. "They're great cupcakes, by the way."

"Are they?" Wes asks, momentarily distracted.

"Yes. Delicious." Right, that was the word I was looking

for earlier. A normal, appropriate word of appreciation for a cake, and you can tell, because Maisie gives a shy, proud smile.

"Damn it, Sev." He sighs.

I grunt an agreement, and take my opportunity. "I need her at Morden. I know you don't like the legal stuff, but I'll tell you what. I'll launder fifteen per cent of your dirt for free, and you give me your daughter."

"As your *employee*," he checks, and I have him.

"She's part of Morden now." And part of me.

There's a pause. "I knew she was unhappy, and wanted to do something, but..." He growls in frustration. "Could she not have waited until I sorted it out?"

"Gen Z has higher expectations due to technological changes and economic uncertainty," I say with a straight face, but Maisie has to cover her mouth with her hand as she giggles.

My frozen heart cracks. What a fucking disaster this is.

"She can stay for now," Wes grumbles. "Guess she might as well be useful, and you'll do a quarter of my cleaning."

"Steep price. She'll live in Morden accommodation so you can't use her as a spy."

Her hands fall away from her mouth and there's an expression of awe on her face.

She wants independence, and I can give it to her. Mafia bosses aren't the most compromising, and while I only found out that Wes had a daughter when he brought it up five years ago, and has barely mentioned her since, I can't imagine it's been fun.

"Temporary," Wes says and slams the phone down.

And just like that, I've won, and lost, all at the same time.

"You saved me," she breathes, her face shining with happiness and she stumbles forward. "Thank—"

"Do not make me out to be a white knight, Miss Matthews," I cut her off. "You will pay for this favour."

For a moment it seems like she might throw herself over the desk to hug me, but she stops short.

My heart clenches. That's good. Better.

She mustn't come near me. She's utterly forbidden, and I don't think I can hold back if I have her within reach.

I imagine her brushing my arm with that small hand, and setting off a trigger of need that ends with her pinned against the wall, or over my desk, my hands pressing into her hips as I force her to take my cock.

"Of course. I'll do anything."

Oh god, I wish she hadn't said that.

"I really need this job. It's my only way of escaping my father's stifling household. I'll be a model worker. No," she casts around, "silliness or cupcakes. You can pay me less." She picks the cupcake tub from the floor with a sheepish look. "I'll work for nothing, in fact."

"No, you'll be paid as appropriate. You're under my protection now." She's my employee, and off-limits.

Her cheeks pinken. "That's really kind of you, Mr Blackwood."

"No, it's not." I don't allow myself to return her smile. That smile isn't for me, just as she isn't for me. I've done some dark things in my life, but this might be the worst. I can't have her, but I must see her. But not face to face.

She'll pay with her privacy.

# 3

# MAISIE

2 YEARS LATER

When will I actually feel like an adult? I look up from my book and cup of tea and glance around at my tiny apartment.

It's a Saturday evening, and I'm—as usual—on my own, and reading. But this book isn't holding my attention, and instead of being engrossed in a world of dragon riders and magic, my thoughts are drifting to my boss.

Specifically, what I'd need to do to make Mr Blackwood view me like the hero of this book does the heroine. As desirable, and an adult. And that reminds me that despite my best efforts, I'm still not out of my father's shadow.

Before I started working for Mr Blackwood, I thought if I got out of Mitcham and had a place of my own and a job, I would feel like a proper grown-up. But no.

I'm still constrained. My father won't permit me to go out with my colleagues, and I dare not push him because his reply will be to revoke his "temporary" permission for me to work, and start talking again about me being a good little mafia princess, and marrying and having kids.

Perhaps this dissatisfaction is because I didn't grow up with my kingpin dad. I barely saw him when I was a kid, and I couldn't believe it when I discovered he was my legal guardian when my mum died.

Since then, it's been a crash course on mafia princess life.

And it's not that I don't want a husband and a baby, it's just that my taste in men is very specific, and I don't think anyone involved would approve of my sad devotion to my grumpy boss. Certainly not Mr Blackwood. Definitely not my father.

But I feel like the best years of my life are passing me by cars on a drizzly Tuesday evening when I'm walking home from work.

I read. I bake cupcakes that my colleagues at Morden appreciate. And even though I don't have the courage to go to offer Mr Blackwood a cupcake, I'm still living off his expression when he ate one two years ago.

I've been thinking about getting a cat.

But sometimes I think there must be more than this. I should be out partying or something, I guess. If only I was allowed friends, party clothes, or knew where to sneak out to in London. With Mr Blackwood, maybe? A date. A real date, with my gorgeous boss. That's what I long for.

Suddenly, I'm itchy. It's a Saturday night, and I'm on my sofa thinking about my boss, who is also my dad's best friend. Talk about pathetic.

Yes, he's attractive, and yes, having him support me against my dad made me unfairly susceptible to his brand of brooding charm. A silver fox, he has grey at his temples and blue eyes that are almost inhuman. He has dark stubble across his square jaw, and a pronounced Adam's apple just above his crisp white shirt collars.

Admittedly, he's the grumpiest man alive. He has a wicked sense of humour though, and he strokes the stray ginger tomcat who hangs out in the Morden Company building.

Handsome, powerful, kind to animals, and murders the men who disrespect women.

Whereas I am a wannabe cat lady, not even owning a real cat myself, and I can't go out at night because my dad would kill anyone who I spent time with, and I'm not mean enough to do that to Trish in accounts. Besides, she's stopped inviting me for evenings with the other girls who work for Morden because I always say no.

I consider browsing the rescue kittens listings.

Or making some cupcakes.

Maybe I need a new book? Everything is solved by a new book… except this hole of loneliness in my chest.

I am a sad, sad case, and I have to shake this up. But while technically I'm an independent adult, my dad is a mafia boss, and I'm not tempted to find out what he'll do if I break his rules.

Okay. Enough.

I put my book aside and stand. I am all alone in my apartment, so I will have a solo party. I've seen movies. I know how this is done.

First, I turn on music. Something upbeat and fun. I strip off my fluffy hoody, then shuck off my yoga pants to reveal my white cotton boy shorts and the little blue vest top.

Shimmying over to the fridge, I slide on the smooth floor. There's one bottle of wine in the otherwise nutritionally empty cold box. I'm not saying I live off cereal, but I guess I live off cereal.

Thankfully it's a screw-top—not by accident—and I wiggle my bottom in time to the music as I pour myself a glass.

I am too boring. I need to loosen up. I take a sip of wine and dance, letting the music flow through me.

I admit, I close my eyes, raise my arms and dance as sexily as I can, thinking how it would feel if Mr Blackwood was watching.

This is fantasy. It's delicious. I can almost feel his eyes on me. I wiggle my bottom. It would be better if it were real. If Mr Blackwood were watching and I was a girl men were interested in. Specifically, my boss was interested in.

Sipping more wine, I boogie around the kitchen. This is fun!

The music switches to a new song and I hum. I don't know all the words, but I don't need to.

I dance through my little apartment. Past my bedroom, and into the lounge, and on a whim, I skip onto the sofa, singing along with the chorus. Exhilarating.

Maybe this is what I've been missing all this time.

I eye up the coffee table. I've got a nice buzz from the wine and the music now, and I'm happy. This is all I need.

Dancing on the table. That's the perfect thing. I've never danced on a table, and today is the day.

I step onto it, between my piles of books, and wiggle, arms out to my sides. In the movies, girls look super cute, and I probably don't. But I'm alone. No cameras or witnesses in sight, so it's fine.

The singer hits a high note, and I pretend to sing it too, striking a pose. And in so doing, I tread on a paperback on the table that I hadn't noticed, and slip.

I fall with all the grace of an over-caffeinated giraffe on ice, shrieking and floundering. My hip hits the floor with a thud, and my head bounces from the edge of the sofa right onto the corner of the coffee table, then to the floor.

I have enough time to feel pain exploding around my eye socket, then a book slides off the sofa and hits me in the face.

Ah, crap.

I lie there for a second, brought low by a coffee table and my paperback addiction.

"Ugh." I pick up the book and peer at the cover.

It's the one that started this whole thing by reminding me of Mr Blackwood and not being entertaining enough.

Clambering to my feet, I look down at myself and shake my head. I even have wine on my white cotton underwear.

Being an adult. Nailed it.

4
―――
SEV




My heart jumps into my throat and I'm on my feet in an instant, as though I'll run over to Maisie's apartment to pick her up, tend her wounds, and comfort her dented pride.

"Maisie. Sweetheart."

I watch as she lies on the floor.

She doesn't move, and that's it. I'm calling an ambulance. I can't stand by if she's really hurt.

Fuck.

One minute you're innocently enjoying watching—alright stalking—the forbidden girl you love more than anything in the world, the next you're in police custody for reporting a domestic incident you should never have known about.

Okay, that would be bad. Adrenaline pumps through my limbs as I grab up my phone and run across my penthouse apartment the size of an aircraft hanger and similarly furnished, flicking on the app for Maisie's cameras. The smaller screen is indistinct for as I reach for the door handle, my car keys in hand.

I'm shaking. Fuck. What am I, a weird aunt?

It's just... She cannot be hurt. Not Maisie.

For my girl to knock herself out and bleed out on her white carpet would be the ultimate irony. Dying because the stalker mafia boss didn't intervene.

So the relief when she moves is beyond anything I've felt. It's life. More intense than my first breath after Camden waterboarded me all those years ago.

I pause, staring at the grainy image. Maisie stands, then flops onto the sofa.

She laughs, and although I can't hear it, I do. Her laughter echoes through me.

I watch her checking every part of her body.

And mine responds with the inevitability of a man starved. I would say that I drool, but it's not usually called that if it's from your cock.

"Fuck." I scrape my hand through my greying hair. I nearly gave myself away.

My girl doesn't have a clue that I love her. She is totally oblivious that my world centres around her.

And as I sink onto the nearest sofa, I close my eyes and remind myself why that is so important. Because Maisie is as off-limits as pizza takeaway for a polar bear. She's half my age, yes. And my employee. Bad. Very bad. And she's the *daughter of my best friend.*

I open my eyes again and watch Maisie find a graze on her leg and wince when she touches her hip.

Quickly, I rewind the tape and pause it at the moment she falls.

All the grace of a cardboard box, my girl, and I adore that about her. I check several times, regarding one frame at a time, and she doesn't hit her head. She'll have a black eye, but no concussion.

Phew. Okay.

Wes would kill me if he knew I watched his daughter with cameras in her own home. But I can't turn away. Maisie is a temptation I can't resist.

She thinks I'm her arsehole boss who snaps at her, but I'm more than that. Worse. I'm her stalker. And every day I watch her, I fall for her more.

For two years.

# 5

## MAISIE

I have a meeting first thing Monday morning with the Blackwood triplets and my dad, and I am aiming for invisibility. Two of the Blackwoods—but not my boss, I'd know—and my dad are in the conference room when I walk in.

Taking a seat, I pray. Sometimes they just get on with business and I take notes and it's—

"What happened to your face, Miss Matthews?" one of the Blackwoods says.

I wince. So much for hoping no one would notice.

"Nothing!" I tip my head down. It's a black eye. Not as bad as the bruise on my bottom, but rather more difficult to hide at work.

"That isn't nothing!" my dad explodes. "Tell me immediately!"

I already have a reputation in Morden for being clumsy —no one has forgotten my cupcake disaster on my first day —and there's no way I'm telling anyone that I was trying to dance on a table, and fell off. Not even a proper table, either. A coffee table.

I have my pride.

"Shark attack," I reply, looking up.

There's a shocked silence, then one of the Blackwood brothers bursts into laughter.

"Vito, that isn't funny." Rafe Blackwood rolls his eyes. "Was the shark a biped?"

"Pretty sure sharks are fish." I try to stare him down, but he's a mafia boss, and I'm really not.

"So, this was a diving incident," Vito drawls. "It is an impressive shiner."

"Should have seen the other guy." The coffee table looks even stupider with those foam corner things than I do with a black eye. Revenge was sweet.

"The shark? I'll nip down to the aquarium," Vito says.

"Was it your boyfriend?" asks Rafe pointedly.

"No!" I'm falling over my own tongue to get that denial out. My dad will go nuts if he thinks I'm dating. I'm blushing, which doesn't help. Because this was all started by my thinking about how much I adore my boss—who doesn't know I exist—and being determined not to be a tragic case.

Great job on that one.

"She doesn't have a boyfriend," Dad growls. "Or if she does, he's twice as dead now."

"Twice as dead? Is this like the 'shark attack'?" Vito grins like he's enjoying this. "We're not playing by the laws of physics anymore."

Oh god.

"I mean that she's the mafia princess of Mitcham, and when she marries it will be because I have arranged it. Any man who touches her before then is dead. And anyone who hurts my daughter is dead as well. Twice dead." My dad says this as though it's totally logical, then turns to me.

"I'll let the shark know," I say brightly.

"So what did this shark look like?" Vito is leaning back in his chair, evidently enjoying this. "Grey? Purple? Blue?"

"Brown, actually." I think I'm now implying I was hit by a table. Or that a table is my boyfriend. Who would be twice dead, if he existed.

I'm so screwed.

Bracing his forearms on the table, my dad pins me with a look that is as ugly and violent as it is protective. "Who hurt you?" He enunciates each word like they're bullets.

"It was..." A table. And a book.

And not in the emotional way books usually hurt people.

They all regard me expectantly.

I cannot say I slipped dancing on a table, on my own. That is too pathetic, even by my standards. My dad will order me home to Mitcham and to stop working here if he thinks my apartment isn't safe. This was a mistake.

I should have thrown a sickie.

"Nothing," I say. "Really."

"Was it a bear?" Vito asks, absolutely straight.

Rafe snorts with laughter.

"Bears are brown," Vito points out.

I think of the table. "Basically, yes."

Dad's brows are so low he'll have to surgically remove them from his legs. I search my mind. What can I say? That isn't too silly, and is plausible.

"I, uh, fell."

There's silence.

"On the stairs." There are no stairs in my apartment. It's all on *one level*. But thankfully no one thinks of this. "It was a stupid accident."

Dad's expression goes worried. "I really think you should go to the hospital—"

My boss sweeps in through the open door, totally at home in the steel and glass, as though he's made of it. His eyes flash as bright-blue as the sky outside.

My heart skips.

Severino Blackwood is so gorgeous, it's almost unreal. He's like a force of nature that you can't ignore, and he's different to his brothers in a way that's obvious to me. Tiny details, like the amount of grey at his temples and the lines around his eyes. His hair is cut differently, and he tends to wear a pale grey suit where his brothers favour charcoal or dark-blue.

He stops abruptly and looks me up and down. A very grumpy wonder of the world.

"A hospital visit, and no more dancing on tables, Miss Matthews," he orders brusquely. "And you lot, stop harassing my staff."

He glowers at his two identical brothers and my dad, and they all accept Mr Blackwood like he's a gloomy cloud of a father figure shutting up bickering children.

He starts the meeting, but there's white noise buzzing around me, thick as soup.

I'm floating above my body as I take a seat at the boardroom table and automatically begin to take notes. I keep my head down, but the shock keeps echoing through me.

*Dancing on a table.*

How did Mr Blackwood know that?

I replay the conversation again, and no. No, I'm sure. I didn't let on about falling off the table. I said stairs. And sharks. And other silly things, but I am one hundred per cent certain that I didn't tell anyone I hurt myself dancing on a table.

So how did he know?

"Miss Matthews?" Mr Blackwood's curt tone breaks through my disbelief.

My head snaps up, and I'm lost in my boss' blue eyes. Again.

"Could I trouble you to write down that address for us, Miss Matthews?" he drawls. "I wouldn't want to disturb your daydreaming, but perhaps you could do your job, please."

It's hardly the worst thing he's ever said to me. Mr Blackwood is notoriously grumpy.

"This address?" I reel off the one they mentioned, and my boss' eyes narrow.

His brothers laugh, but I hold Mr Blackwood's gaze.

"Oh, she just owned you, Sev," my dad says.

But I'm watching my boss. There's something inexplicably proud in his expression. Like he's impressed.

"Very good, Miss Matthews."

Tension sizzles between us for one second, then two, as Vito speaks, and I really am not listening this time. I'm looking into Sev Blackwood's face and the only thought in my head, is *how*? How did he know?

He growls at me regularly, and I've always assumed he didn't like me, and that my crush was totally one-sided. But I'm wondering now. I live in a property owned by Mr Blackwood, and I have since I started working here.

There's only one way my boss could know I hurt myself dancing on a table, since I don't look like the kind of girl who does that. If he saw it happen.

# 6
## SEV

I only see her once during the rest of the workday, and I snap at her, "Why aren't you having that eye sorted out?"

I am an unmitigated arsehole.

And when I open my phone to the surveillance app after the little blue dot on the tracker shows me she's at home, I breathe a sigh of relief.

I settle down with a glass of Scotch and my tablet to an evening of my favourite pastime—stalking Maisie.

It's more fun to follow her in person, but it's a weekday night, and my brothers have only just finished giving me shit. I wonder what my girl is doing?

I flick to the surveillance app with a smile, and anticipation in my heart. I love watching her read, or...

My jaw falls open. I cannot believe what I'm seeing. Maisie's usual attire once she's home from work is a slouchy T-shirt and yoga pants, with her hair in a haphazard ponytail. She relaxes on the sofa, and reads on that little digital thing, and eats cereal or something from the microwave.

But not tonight. This evening, Maisie has chosen violence towards her hidden audience of one.

She's wearing a tiny negligee. I can see her tits peeking out from the cleavage, and the tops of her thighs are tantalisingly just in view.

She's reading a book, but that's the only familiar aspect of this.

I know her reading tastes are what is sometimes called "fairy porn", and that's not totally inaccurate having read some of it myself, but honestly anyone who has watched porn knows that you don't have to wade through eight hundred pages of battling monsters and cheek touches to get to the good stuff. There is no comparison.

And she has just started this series. It's unlikely it's this horny on page twelve.

Part of me wants to download the book she's reading right now to find out, but another part of me—my cock, specifically—demands that I remain where I am.

A drink, a view of the woman I love, and a huge empty penthouse. I guess this is as good as it gets.

My cock hardens as Maisie gets comfortable on the sofa, but my mind gets stuck, as it sometimes does, particularly when I've seen my brothers. She looks hot. Maisie is my ideal masturbation material.

But I don't touch myself yet, because my heart aches. I wish she were here.

My elder brothers both have wives, and children on the way. They have love and laughter and companionship, and I am fucking jealous. When it was just Rafe that was bad enough. But now it's Vito too—only months after I got him back from Milan—and the contrast makes the feeling even more stark.

I'm lonely. In the past I got a kick out of sabotaging Rafe, giving Vito shit about his accent, breaking the fingers of some ticker who overstepped, or finding an especially good planning loophole.

I used to find joy in watching Maisie. It was enough for so long. And past me is delighted that she is wandering around in a see-through dress. Negligee. Whatever.

But now I'd give everything to have Maisie with me, fully clothed.

And I can't. My best friend would be as accepting of me being with his daughter as a pigeon is of clean cars.

So although my desire for Maisie is far from only physical, I keep it that way. This is more than I dreamed of, in fact.

Maisie on the screen is adjusting her position as she reads, and the front of that little tease of fabric flops down, giving me a perfect view of her tits.

And yeah, I crave her company.

But I'm a man. I want her lush, tight body, as well as her soul.

Then she eases one hand down her stomach, and I stop breathing as she reaches into her lace knickers.

She's touching herself. Then she's writhing, and the book is cast aside, and somehow, she's looking straight up into the camera as she goes pink in the cheeks and her mouth opens in a pant of desire.

Suddenly, it's too much. I rip open my trousers and release my cock, then jerk myself. Using my left hand, it feels slightly less like it's me, and I can imagine it's her. Inexperienced, but eager as she can't wrap her fingers all the way around.

My cock is thick and heavy with need. I stroke myself with quick, harsh pumps of my fist as I watch. The pleasure is sharp, and I throw back the last of my whisky as I feel the tingle as my balls fill up, telling me I'm close.

Breathing hard, I take my hand off my cock and flick my shirt buttons open, revealing the familiar lines of the tattoos that cover my chest.

On the screen, Maisie has altered position, so her arse is pointed straight into the camera as she bends at the waist and continues to stroke her clit inside the knickers.

"Fuck," I breathe. "It's like you're trying to make me think of taking you that way, Maisie."

It's not.

She doesn't know I'm watching.

I don't have any illusions about myself, but when Maisie arches her back and wiggles her arse, I feel like the filthy monster I truly am.

I stroke one thumb delicately over the screen, wishing I could touch her. Then when she shakes and collapses as she comes, I blow my load in wild spurt after spurt. Uncontrolled.

It's pleasurable. And hollow.

---

She continues like this. Walking around in her apartment in hardly any clothes—just a pair of white cotton knickers, or a baggy T-shirt that doesn't cover her arse. Sometimes only wearing tiny knickers.

It's like she's deliberately teasing me. I've been stalking Maisie for two years, and she's a young woman with the usual needs, but they've been satisfied in her bed before. Now, she reclines on the sofa and flicks the bean, with or without underwear, or sits on the kitchen counter. Her bruises heal, and she looks more beautiful and sexy by the day.

If watching her was good before, it's somewhere around torture now. It used to be an obsession, it's turned into an addiction.

So it's a positive thing when I have a social appointment where I absolutely cannot open my phone and sneak a look at Maisie.

Wes and I meet in the Morden executive exercise suite, the part that actually has a gym and a shooting range, not the cells. They've been thoroughly cleaned, and are thankfully empty of distractions. Wes is far too bloodthirsty to focus on target practise or lifting weights when there's someone to extract information from.

We're chatting about London mafia politics and trying out some new guns Wes has had shipped in, when he changes the subject.

"I've been thinking about Maisie. I'm still concerned about that bruise she had. What if she has a boyfriend?"

I choke slightly. "She doesn't have a boyfriend."

"How do you know?"

"Because I'd kill him." I pull the trigger repeatedly, with more force than necessary. It's a blanket denial of the idea of Maisie being with anyone, as well as a rejection of the link to her self-inflicted bruise.

Wes nods. "You said you'd look after her, and I trust you."

And I'm betraying that trust by watching his daughter touch herself. Intimately. And doing a bit of a follow-along myself. If my best friend knew, I'd be dead in seconds.

Cheery thought.

"How's Maisie getting on at work?" Wes fires off a round at the moving target. "How long has she been at Morden now?"

My chest is tight as I flick new ammunition into my pistol and avoid looking at him.

"Dunno," I lie.

"Surely she's bored? She has that business degree, but I can't think she uses it?"

I shrug. She's been promoted multiple times and is a junior manager, but I doubt Wes will appreciate that.

"I don't see her much." Also a lie. "Just when she takes notes, or meetings. Like for our South London cabal sessions. It's good having a trustworthy person around."

"I wish she would work for me," he grumbles. "Or do her duty as a mafia princess and marry for the benefit of Mitcham."

"She can marry me, if you ask really nicely," I say in my usual dry manner.

"I will kill you if you touch her," he replies, emptying his whole clip into the target.

"If you shoot me with that much accuracy, I'll marry your son and your dog, too," I smirk.

"I'll murder you with a spoon." He slams the next clip in with unnecessary force. "Heard it hurts more that way."

"She's twenty-three years old. You're upset she doesn't eat with a spoon anymore, so you feel old." I keep my tone light and cynical, hiding how much this means to me.

"Fuck you," Wes spits. "I'm closer to twenty-three than she is."

I laugh. "Same."

"Thanks for looking out for her. I just can't accept she's grown up," he grumbles. "My daughter is a baby."

"With a full-time job," I point out.

"Child labour."

"You were telling me I'm going soft. Child labour seems the kind of thing I could get behind."

We're walking a tightrope.

"Morally corrupt is fine." Wes gives me a look that turns my blood cold. "But nobody touches my daughter."

# 7
## SEV

"Miss Matthews to see you," my assistant, Nathan, says when I pick up the phone.

Shit.

It's been over a week since Maisie has been indulging in self-love and posing semi-naked every evening, and I'm beginning to wear thin on restraint, so I've been avoiding her at work.

My brow furrows.

This is fine. I can keep control of myself.

Probably.

"Send her in."

"Mr Blackwood?" A few seconds later, she timidly peeks around the door as though I might turn her away.

I don't return her bright, hopeful smile, and just flick my fingers to indicate she should enter.

"It's about the report on the Parkside development. I printed it and brought it to you."

My brain is so taken up with the fact she's in my office looking fresh and beautiful as a summer day that I only nod at the spurious pretext. I hate reading on paper, and always have things emailed.

She closes the door and smooths her skirt down nervously. She's wearing a fussy little blouse and a flicky skirt in a deep-blue.

It's pure torture to see and not peel those clothes from her body. What makes it even worse is watching her choose the outfit in the morning and put it on, then wear it never knowing I've seen it already, and see her take it off again. All without touching her.

Maisie comes to stand before my desk and I—as ever—think of bending her over my desk and fucking her until she's come at least three times, and we're both exhausted.

I manage to restrain myself.

Another successful day as a stalker.

"What can I do for you?" I ask mildly. I sit back and don't quite look her in the eye, like she's the sun. "Something to do with your father?"

It's good to remind myself of why she's so off-limits; that she could be wrapped in that white and red plastic caution tape that says "do not enter", "danger of death", and "these orgasms will literally kill you".

That seems to jolt her, and she blinks. Then my innocent girl licks her lips. "Mr Blackwood, I need your help."

Adrenaline surges in me. She needs me? I'm there.

If this is about a photocopier, I'm going to be really disappointed.

"Something to do with work?"

"Sort of." She gives a half giggle, nervous and breathy.

There's no chair on the other side of my desk, because I don't encourage my visitors to stay too long, as a rule. So I have the torture of seeing her shift from foot to foot. I'd like to make her comfortable. Instead, I have this mask of sour temper and callous disregard for anyone's feelings, but since she's been in my life the mask itches and chafes, and part of me wishes I could remove it.

Not with her. I can't take off the mask with Maisie. I can only be the beast. The stalker. The bad man hiding in the shadows.

Just like loneliness doesn't wash off, the mask of indifference can't slip.

"Go on," I say, when she hesitates.

"You know my father doesn't allow me to go out?"

I give a single nod. A totally reasonable rule.

"I want some experience of life." She looks up at me with those doe eyes and I can feel the slippery slope argument.

"Mmm." What has this got to do with me?

"And since you helped me with a job, I thought you might help me with this too. I'm not asking you to let me go out in London, or anything like that. But you could do this. Yourself."

"What is 'this', Miss Matthews?" I rumble. But I know. The sight from last night is tattooed onto my retinas as surely as the symbols of Morden are tattooed onto my skin.

My girl is horny.

Still, I hold my breath.

"I've never been kiss—"

"No," I respond before she even finishes saying the word.

She's never been kissed? My cock responds to that with the inevitability of a cartoon character running off a cliff then looking down.

She's not kissing anyone when she's under my protection, because it's me, or no one.

So it's no kisses for the girl with lips meant to be kissed and used for sin.

"Absolutely not," I add when she doesn't reply, licking her bottom lip with that soft pink tongue.

"Please," she says, in a breathy little pant. "I've been feeling restless recently, and I can't think of anyone I trust more, Mr Blackwood."

"No."

"Just one kiss?" she wheedles. "I really need a lesson. An experienced man to teach me how to kiss."

I'm dizzy. This isn't happening, and yet, it is. First, she played into all my fantasies by revealing herself to me on camera—unknowingly—and now she says she wants me to introduce her to kissing?

"Your father would kill me if he finds I've given you kissing lessons."

"No one ever needs to know," she says, as though it's that simple.

"Your father trusts me."

"That's why you're the perfect person to help!" she insists. "I trust you too, and you're old enough to know what you're doing."

I should say no. Me giving kissing lessons to Maisie is like a tiger teaching a rabbit how to cook a steak. She's too tempting.

This will end in disaster.

"Or should I ask someone else at work?" she suggests innocently. "Who do you think? Maybe the young guy in—"

"No." My fists clench. "No. That isn't..."

That's not acceptable because Maisie belongs to me.

"I have a duty of care to all my employees," I say. "If someone is going to be killed for kissing you, it's me."

That's a convenient excuse that conceals that I would murder anyone else who kissed Maisie myself.

"Great!" She gives me that distinctive sunny smile. I don't return it because I think my heart might beat right out of my chest. "How do we start?"

Now?

Fuck, obviously now. But I need a bit more time to emotionally prepare myself for life-threatening acts like having my dream of the last two years come true.

"Over here, Maisie." My voice is hoarse. I push my chair back and pray that my erection doesn't cause too many issues as I rise and walk to the sofa on the side of my office closest to the window. It looks out over Morden, high enough to see but not be seen from any other building. Sinking onto the yielding leather, I beckon her with one finger.

"Yes, Mr Blackwood—"

"Sev. My name is Severino." I drag in a shaky breath. "If I'm going to kiss you, you should call me by that name."

"Sev," she repeats softly.

My brain helpfully conjures up the image of the sound of her saying my name as I sink into her soaking pussy.

She skips over towards me, though it's not exactly a skip —she's not five years old—but there's a spring in her step like this is a delightful, cute activity like collecting wildflowers and singing innocent songs.

Not approaching her grumpy and obsessive stalker boss.

Her flicky little skirt teases around her legs as she rounds my desk and takes her place beside me, placing the stack of papers on the low table.

"What now?" She glances up through her long dark lashes.

This is going to kill me. She's slight, soft, curved, and

small compared to me. The scent of raspberries and cream fills my senses.

I look into her eyes. Up close, they're endless shades of brown, as though her genetics got over-zealous as a mafia boss buying a present for his wife, and gave her every colour imaginable, all mushed together.

"Your first kiss, huh?"

"Yes." She leans in to press her lips to mine hurriedly.

"Uh!" I'm not having that. An awkward, quick kiss that leaves her as unsatisfied as me. My hand finds her waist, and holds her.

"What?" She pulls back reluctantly, hurt in her expression.

"I thought you said you wanted to be taught?" I rumble.

She nods, her eyebrows puckering together.

"Then let me teach, sweetheart." The endearment falls out of my mouth far too easily. "First you need to set up the cause for the kiss," I murmur. "Look at this with me." Picking up a paper from the coffee table at random, I place it between us. "See here?"

"I don't see," she replies, a bit confused.

"Come closer then. Lean in." I'm a monster luring his soft little prey.

"You see the point I'm trying to teach you?" I put one finger onto the page. "Just here?"

"This one?" She puts a fingertip next to mine.

There's the thud of my heart, the wind outside, and someone talking downstairs.

"That's right. A bit closer."

"Do you mean..." Her finger brushes over mine as she indicates another place on the page.

The lurch of my stomach is almost painful. This smallest of all touches is the most I've had in two years.

"That's it. Clever girl." Miraculously, my voice remains calm. Unaffected, even. "But I think you'll find..." I shift and run my index finger down hers. She's smooth and warm and it's the strangest contradiction. I'm having difficulty controlling myself and want to yank her onto my lap, shove our clothes aside, and take her. But at the same time, I'm relishing this perfect moment we're creating.

It's so good, I'm almost fooled by it myself.

And the danger is undeniably hot. The unlocked door—even if Nathan knows better than to enter unannounced, or allow anyone else to—is precarious. We could be caught, and it makes the excitement of our age gap, and the forbidden nature of this all the hotter.

"Sev," she whispers and looks up at me.

"Good, now tilt your chin up in an invitation. Offer me your lips."

She makes a soft whimper as she does as I say.

"Now open your mouth for me, just a little."

Her dusky pink lips part.

"Good girl."

My cock throbs so intensely I might pass out from lack of blood in my brain. That's clearly the reason I'm doing this. Toying with a risk that will result in death from my best friend.

But I don't care that he's my best friend now. I can't understand why she's my employee. She's my obsession, and my inner monster has already claimed her as my wife. All the rest is details that will be sorted out in time.

Or not.

"I'm looking at your lips because I want them crushed to mine," I say hoarsely.

"Should I look at your lips too?" she asks, a little shy.

"You can."

Seeing her eyeline drop sends a surge of anticipation through me. As though she craves this as much as I do.

It's just a lesson, I remind myself.

"The tension that is undeniable," I whisper. "Feel how inevitable it is that we're going to give in to the scorching attraction between us."

Nathan answers the phone on the other side of the door, muffled and indistinct.

"Can you feel how the taboo makes it hotter? The sounds of Nathan just a layer of wood away, and the risk of getting caught?"

"Mr Blackwood," she whispers, and leans in further, our lips only inches apart now.

Who is seducing who here?

Wait, no. I'm supposed to be teaching her.

"Do you like that I'm your boss? Does it make you feel powerful that I want you? That despite billions in the bank and a small army for the Morden mafia, I'm looking at you like you're the only thing that matters in the world, and I'm tortured by not being able to have you?"

I don't mention her father. That shimmers between us without words.

"Because you're so young, Maisie. I shouldn't kiss you."

"You should," she whispers back, and her breath is warm and sweet on my lips. "You can take whatever you want."

I groan. "Don't say that." I don't think I can hold it together if she says things like that. I might believe her. "Say that you'd like a kiss. Just one, to be taught."

"Sev, kiss me. Please."

Touching a finger to her jaw I shift closer. Her scent—raspberries and cream—fills my senses.

"I shouldn't, Maisie. I'm twice your age. I'm your boss."

"Please." It's a broken little word, and it breaks me too.

I groan and guide her mouth to mine, giving her a butterfly of a kiss. The sort of kiss that is an expression of lust and longing in the form of a carefully deniable brush that could have been an accident.

Her cheek is so soft. She's delicate and small and I try to be exactly the sweet first kiss that she deserves. I drag my lips over hers and everything in me tightens when I hear her needy little gasp.

"What should I do?" she murmurs. "I don't know how to do this right."

"We should stop," I say, but I don't. I catch her lower lip, and venture the tip of my tongue against her lips.

"Sev," she gasps.

"Open your mouth more," I instruct her. "And angle your head."

She does exactly as I say. And despite all the reasons to hurry, I tempt and lure, still holding her cheek lightly as though it's not costing me my sanity.

"Now slowly, use the moments between my lips moving, and repeat what I do." It's taking everything in me to keep up the pretence that I'm her impassive teacher.

I'm not. I'm a monster.

I deepen the kiss by fractions, drawing her in bit by bit. And she responds with all the innocent understanding of the girl meant to learn from me. She's a quick study, turning my tricks on me and nipping at my lower lip when I allow a tiny break in my domination of the kiss.

I keep her at a careful distance, even as I begin to plunder her mouth, my hand moving to the back of her head. Her hair is black silk, just as I always knew it would be.

"Good girl. You're doing so well."

We're kissing in earnest now, and she's doing what I can't. Pulling us together, wriggling and shifting closer, looping her arms around my shoulders.

"I can't breathe without you," I confess hoarsely.

This might be all I ever get, and although it's more than I've dreamed Maisie would be interested in, I'm just a man. My cock is so hard it's straining against my belt, and I'm pretty sure the leaking pre-come has soaked through my boxers.

All from one kiss.

"Sev," she whispers, and I'm undone.

The intercom buzzes. Nathan's trying to contact me.

I ignore it and grab Maisie's waist—so small—with my free hand and in a second she's fully on my lap. At the back of my mind, I know there's a reason this is wrong.

Forbidden.

But with Maisie—finally, finally—in my arms, I can't think over the sheer rightness. I kiss her harder, torn between running my hands up her sides, and holding her possessively. Tight, like I might never let her go. She moans, rubbing her thigh against my cock, shooting pleasure all the way through me.

"Mr Blackwood." There's a rapid knock on the door, then the muffled sound of Nathan's raised voice. "Westminster is here to see you. He's a bit ahead of time."

Fuck. How could I have forgotten about that meeting with Westminster of all people?

We break the kiss, both breathing heavily and our gazes meet. Maisie's pupils are blown wide, and a rapid pulse flutters at her throat. She shifts on my lap, her thigh pressing onto my cock.

My entirely hard cock, that jumps at the touch, even through layers of our clothing.

I was wrong. *This* is going to kill me. Stopping now, when all I want is to continue until my come is leaking out of her and she's liquid from multiple orgasms.

"Tell him I'll be there in a minute," I say, loudly enough to be heard through the solid door.

"That's..." She wriggles slightly on my lap.

I bite back a groan. "That's what happens when you kiss a man."

"Me?" There's awe in her tone, and she's going to break me. Teaching this girl? Pretending that I'm just kissing her because she's asked me to and not because I crave her? Impossible.

"You have no idea the danger you're in, sweetheart," I mutter as I lift her off me and onto her feet, ensuring she's steady before I let her go.

I force my gaze from her and rearrange my trousers to make my hard-on less obvious.

"How do I look?" she asks anxiously, smoothing her hair and clothes down, and adjusting her top. She touches her bee-stung pink lips.

Fuckable.

Like she's been kissed and is wet between the legs, and ready.

Perfect. Beautiful.

Except there's a stray tendril of hair sticking up from when I plunged my hand into it like I want to thrust my cock into her sweet cunt.

I reach out and unhook it, then run my fingertips down so it's neat. I long to tell her that she looks like she should be my wife, and stay by my side as I talk mafia politics, and come to my bed every night all soft and warm.

Instead, I fold my arms and turn away.

"That's the end of your lesson." It's physically painful,

as though my heart is suspended in mid-air, bloodied and torn from my chest by her being further from me. "We can't risk anything getting back to your dad."

I sit behind my desk, roll my shoulders, and then force myself to do the one thing I most don't want to do, that is usually natural to me: sound like a grumpy, uncaring bastard.

"Open the door, and go to leave," I say softly, meeting her eyes.

She nods, still looking like a girl who has been well-kissed. My gaze drops to her arse as she walks across the room, away from me for what I know should be—will be—forever.

When Maisie is about to step out of the office, I set off the trap.

"Miss Matthews."

She halts in the doorway, instinctively obedient, and glances over her shoulder.

"Don't forget your report. Do I need to call Nathan to help you carry it?" I point at the stack of documents she brought to my office as a pretext. "Next time, save the trees and email me your typo-ridden ramblings. Upholding quaint out-of-date traditions like print doesn't make you seem older, or credible. It's just a fucking waste."

"Harsh," Westminster says, audible through Nathan's office.

For a second I see her hurt, and confusion.

*That's it*, I urge her with my eyes. *Get annoyed. Make them think that pink in your cheeks is because you're angry. Or humiliated. They won't even notice how you're scurrying from a private meeting looking as though you've been ravished.*

But instead, she does the one thing I don't expect.

Maisie tilts up her chin, just as I taught her to invite my kiss, and smiles. "Yes, Mr Blackwood. Thank you for that, Mr Blackwood."

Then she grabs the report, and sashays away from my office to Westminster's slow clap.

No one suspects.

## 8

## MAISIE

"I need another lesson," I say to Mr Blackwood when I finally see him in the corridor a week later. And when I say need, I mean it. I am chronically horny from that one kiss.

Can you die from sexual frustration and longing? Only days ago, I'd have said don't be ridiculous. I'd have pointed out that even though it feels like all your blood is in your groin, it's not true. That yeah, it's difficult to think when you're distracted, but surely you just need to focus.

I cannot. It's impossible. And finally, finally, I've found Sev, who has been notably absent from the office since our kiss.

I trot to keep up with him.

"I'm afraid that won't be possible, Miss Matthews," he says coldly, not breaking his stride.

"Right, but it is," I insist.

He accelerates. I do too. We're practically running down the corridor towards the conference room where there will be a meeting between him and his two triplet brothers. And my father.

He has much longer legs than me, and in about ten

paces we'll reach the corner, and be within sight of the door to the conference room.

I have to do something. Anything.

There's a store cupboard, and I take my chance. I grab Sev, yank him to the side with all my strength—he barely moves but growls, "Maisie", and push at the door. Then I drag him into the tiny space and press the door closed behind us.

Sev sighs as he looks down at me. An automatic light has come on, a flickering blue-white bulb with all the romance of an interrogation room. There are piles of flipcharts, boxes of pens, power cords, and shelves with computer equipment haphazardly piled onto them around us. The aesthetic is corporate torture chamber.

"Maisie, we can't do this." He drags his hands through his hair and even under these lights the silver at his temples gleams, and his blue eyes are dark. Almost rings of navy.

I recognise through the dizzying feel of nearness, that he is holding back.

"Please," I say brokenly, gazing up at him, my hand still on his arm from getting him in here.

I can't live without him. I've strip-teased every night since he taught me to kiss, and I felt his erection.

I did that to him. He wanted more, but he's avoided me.

"I need you..."

His frown deepens and something in me breaks.

"No one else will help, because they're scared of my dad. I can't even go out." That's part of the truth, but not all. I only want *him*. "One more lesson. Please."

He's impassive, but he hasn't moved away. He's a statue, unmoving, too still. But his lips twitch, as though there's an interior fight behind a stone wall of his skin.

I step closer, so my breasts touch his middle, and my

neck is craned up to see his face. He's breathing hard, and so am I.

Heat blooms between my legs.

He shudders, the inner struggle finally showing.

"I need more lessons," I whisper and slowly bring my hands to rest on his warm chest. His pale grey suit and impeccable tie are pristine. What is he like underneath all that restraint? His shoulders are broad, and the little I felt of him last time was solid muscle. "I'm begging you."

There's a tense silence.

I have all the smarts of that computer monitor in the corner. Maybe I'm imagining this spark between us? I've dragged my billionaire boss into a store cupboard and I'm groping him.

Perhaps he doesn't want me and there's another explanation for how he knew about me dancing on the table.

My hands fall away and my chin dips. Tears nudge behind my eyes.

Then Sev groans, and before I know it, he's pulled me against the wall with his body.

"Fuck it."

He grips my hair, tugging it so I look at him.

"You want to be taught about sex? This is what you should know, sweetheart." The bar of his cock digs into my soft belly, so hard it almost hurts. "It's risky to play with a man. He might decide to take everything your pretty eyes offer."

The shiver of arousal that goes through me is indecent. My breath is in little pants.

"Or he could shut you up by filling your mouth with his cock instead, fucking your throat until tears run down your cheeks."

Then his lips are on mine again, before I can say that

I'm eager to do what he just said. That I would happily do that and more for him.

This isn't a sweet kiss like before. There's no holding back. He kisses me like he's a wild monster, backing me against the wall until I'm trapped between the cold unyielding plaster and his solid heat.

"Is this what you wanted to experience?" He grinds his erection into me, only thin layers of fabric between us. "A man desperate for you?"

His cock is a hot iron rod digging into me, hurting almost, but it's good pain. It forces a needy whimper from my chest.

"And you want another kiss," he asks, pulling back and glowering down into my face.

"Yes." I tilt my chin up in invitation.

"Then I get to choose where the next kiss is, sweetheart," he replies, and it's so low and full of danger and promise that I shiver.

"Sit there." But before I can move to the boxes he indicates, he's grabbed me by the waist and put me onto them. For a second, I'm a doll. I'm just the weight of a feather as Mr Blackwood lifts me.

He stands between my dangling feet and types a message with impatient taps of his fingers and half his attention, as he shares his gaze between the phone and me. Then he slips the device back into his pocket.

"Told them I'd be late," he informs me tersely. "Now. Lift your skirt."

Fear spikes in me. This isn't like last time, when he charmed and seduced me. This is a demand by a powerful man, who is used to getting his own way.

What will he think if I say no? Or worse, yes.

My hands are on the hem of my dress without my volition. It's as though, despite the sparks of worry—someone might catch us, someone could see, he might think I'm a slut—I trust my boss so entirely I can't fathom not doing what he says. My body knows that I'm his, even as my mind squeaks that this wasn't what I asked for.

He breathes heavily through his nose as I lift my skirt up.

And up. And up. He's so big, it's intimidating revealing myself at his command. Then it's at my waist, and I can't go further.

"Good girl." The praise reverberates through me like a long high note in a song. His gaze sweeps over my plain white cotton panties, his gaze going dark. Then he grasps the lace elastic of the waistband. Dragging it down, he rasps, "Lift."

I shuffle my bottom as best I can to let him pull them off.

He slides them efficiently off my legs and stuffs them into his pocket.

"Your next lesson is to take what I give you and be very quiet, so we aren't caught." He grips my neck and pulls my face to his, his breath ghosting over my lips. "Do you understand?"

I nod eagerly.

"Spread."

I hesitate. That's so embarrassing. So bad. So naughty.

"Now," he grunts. "We don't have much time before my nosey brothers come looking for us."

My muscles almost creak as I part my thighs.

"Yes. More." Then he's dropped to his knees before me and pushes my legs wider apart, until I'm completely open and exposed.

And I would feel terrible, ashamed, my face heating, but

Sev looks at the slit between my legs as though it's food, water and shelter, and he's a man starving after a month alone in the desert. A year. More. A lifetime.

"Maisie," he groans. "So beautiful."

Before I can reply, he's pressing kisses all the way around my core, so passionate that any denial dies in my throat. He's fervent. It's shocking how keen he is. I'm slightly confused, then he gets to my slit.

"Perfectly juicy, and wet," he growls, and gives me a lick that makes my whole body jerk with pleasure.

Footsteps echo down the hallway just outside the door and I tense. But Sev doesn't seem to care, holding my thighs down.

"Fucking delicious." His mouth covers my clit, and I let out an involuntary shriek as a shower of sparks flies from where he sucks me.

"Shh." He gives a rumbling chuckle and reaches up to tweak my waist in punishment. "Quiet girls get orgasms."

"What do...?" I don't manage to ask the question because his tongue finds my clit and it's like nothing I've ever felt. He eats me greedily and my whole focus narrows to this amazing man and what he's doing between my legs.

That and the answer he didn't give to my non-question, but my mind supplies from what he said earlier—bad girl who is too noisy might get her mouth stuffed with his cock.

I can't deny the thought makes me even hotter as Sev works my pussy as though he owns it. He sneaks in his fingers too, first just touching my entrance, then pushing in, insistent.

"Yield for me," he murmurs when I tense, and I do. His fingers—more than one, I think—sink deeply into me and the sensation of having that bulk inside me is magical.

Unreal. It's like having him to struggle against, or perhaps with, makes every stroke of his tongue even better.

It's all I can do to sit upright. I'm slumped, panting. On a stack of cardboard boxes, in a supply cupboard, Sev undoes me, making my body his own. Lighting me on fire.

A door slams somewhere, but my brain can't comprehend what that means or why I should notice. I'm lost, overwhelmed.

"That's it, good girl," he says between licks. "Come for me."

His fingers go demanding. A curl, a beckon. His mouth claps onto my clit and my orgasm is dragged out of me.

I completely lose it. I'm barely aware of who I am, or where we are, as the pleasure cascades through me in pulse after pulse.

Sev is my rock in the storm as bliss tingles right down to my fingertips and toes, radiating out from where he's touching me.

His blue eyes are the first thing I see when my mind and body begin to recover.

His hand is over my mouth, and his middle finger is over my tongue like a pacifier. He's watching me intently, and his lips and cheeks are wet. From licking me, I realise, and a fresh wave of arousal sweeps down my spine.

"Oh hey, have you got the cameras?" The woman's voice is right outside the door, and Sev and I both freeze.

"How many do we need?" I recognise Florence, the head of HR.

"Only ten." That's Trish.

Sev glances from side to side, as I try to shove my shirt back down. But he doesn't move.

"They're going to come in," I hiss, terror flaring down

my spine. He just crowds closer to me, blocking the view of me from a potentially open door.

"Sev." I'm panicking.

"Oh, then we have enough," Florence replies. There's a heart-sinking moment when I'm convinced they'll enter. But they don't, and seconds later another door has opened and closed, and we're alone.

Safe. For now.

Sev hasn't looked away from my face even for a second, like I'm the centre of his world.

Then he snaps and his hands are in my hair and he's kissing me. Desperate, wet, his fingers tugging my sensitive scalp. I taste my own salty sweetness on his tongue, and I moan.

As quickly as he grabbed me, he jerks back, his eyes blaze.

"This cannot happen again."

"But I—"

"No!" His voice is like granite.

"I could—" Do for him what he did for me. And more.

"Clean up," he interrupts me. "Be in the meeting room in five minutes."

Then I'm left staring at the closed door, and I'm broken. A moment ago, it was from white-hot pleasure, but now it's a break that's bloody and cold and dark.

He doesn't want to do this again?

He'll watch me from afar, but he doesn't want the real me.

# 9

## SEV

Fuck. I wipe my face surreptitiously as I walk out of the store cupboard, and duck into the gents to finish cleaning up. I don't look myself in the eyes. I can't.

I lost control. Well. Almost.

I didn't fuck her until she came on my cock, so I suppose I get a gold star for restraint on that count.

Genuinely, I deserve a medal for not taking her right there. Claiming her. My erection is an iron testament to my good behaviour. Practically a monument.

I breathe in deeply as I wash my hands and wipe my face with cold water. A brief re-adjustment and I'm as suitable for company as I'm ever likely to be.

My brothers, Rafe and Vito, and Wes Matthews, are lounging in the conference room at the end of the hallway, and glance up at me when I walk in.

I shouldn't look them in the face, and I recognise my mistake as soon as I make it. I didn't want to see the guilt reflected back at me from the mirror, and my brothers' identical eyes are just as bad.

"Sev." Wes greets me with a nod.

"Have you murdered one of the staff again?" Vito asks.

I mean... In a sense, yes.

"Why were you late? What have you done?" Rafe shakes his head wearily.

"You'll have to find out in your own time, as usual. Information couriered by glacier, no?"

"Does he send spies to work for you, as well?" Wes asks my brothers.

"It's practically a sign of affection from Sev." Vito turns to Wes. "He's done it to all of us."

"A new spy, maybe?" Rafe muses to Vito, totally ignoring me. "I think there's that shifty expression that's a giveaway."

"Shall we talk business, or would you prefer to waste time in speculation about my greatness? I'm good with either." I take a seat at the table.

"Can't start without our note taker," Vito says. "Where is she?"

"Delayed. But we can—" The door opens, and Maisie steps in with a bright smile, that I immediately see is brittle.

I did that. I am a fuckwit.

I've been so desperate since our first kiss though. I've sat in a car outside of her building every night, just for the sensation of being near her. I followed her on the weekend when she went shopping, and watch her on my phone when she's at home.

"Sorry I'm late." She takes the seat beside me, and even as I will us both to not do anything, she glances at me, and I look at her because I'm base metal and she's a magnet.

The zap of electricity is almost audible.

For the split-second I'm looking into her eyes, all I can think of is how she looked as she came. How she tasted.

How much I long to feel her come every day for the rest of my life.

I drag my gaze away to see Rafe and Vito exchange a look.

I glower at them. "Shall we get on?"

"What was the delay?" Rafe asks Maisie innocently.

"Teaching problem," I say.

"Surveillance issue," she replies at the same time.

"Teaching session on how to use the new surveillance software ran over," I cover up smoothly. Maisie is blushing a little as though she's still feeling my tongue between her legs, but covering it with a smile and efficiently tapping at her tablet. I look over at Wes, who is frowning at his daughter. But he's not looking at me. I don't know whether I'm relieved he doesn't suspect anything, or furious that he dares scrutinise Maisie.

She's mine.

Except she's not.

"Surveillance," Vito repeats with sarcasm so heavy it has its own gravitational pull and moon.

"Yes. And luckily for you I'll help with your shitty security problems," I say. "I've got an update on the joint laundering."

Immediately my brothers and my friend are distracted by what Morden offers—the most efficient money laundering in London.

It's only about an hour of meeting, but I'm aware of Maisie for every minute of it. Each second that ticks past my skin is tighter for not being pressed to her. Sometimes I think I can taste her. Smell her.

Raspberries and cream.

"I'd like a quick word with you, Maisie," Wes says as we wrap up. I watch out of the corner of my eye.

"I can't right now, Dad, sorry," she replies with a sunny smile, and neatly packs up her tablet. She's a bit flustered. Could be because she came on my face not that long ago, but my instincts say it's something else.

Wes scowls and I feel simultaneously sorry for him, and relieved because I'm not ready for my best friend to ask his innocent daughter difficult questions about teaching or surveillance.

Wes follows Maisie out of the room, and I stand, helpless to do anything but follow. Even though he is her father, my protective instinct with Maisie is irrepressible.

"Sit down," Rafe orders in his, "I'm the eldest" voice.

"Haven't you got jobs and families to go to?" I snap, ignoring him. They have both. Wives they are having children with, and successful mafias.

"Thankfully for you, we also have family responsibilities of a fraternal kind," Vito says, pushing me back into my chair.

"Is that a type of Italian mushroom?" I glare up at him.

"No, it's the kindness to tell you to stop eating hallucinogenic mushrooms that make you think messing around with Wes Matthew's daughter is a good idea." Rafe rolls his eyes. "Have you regressed to having the survival instincts of mould?"

Oh. Shit.

"I don't know what you're talking about."

"She's the girl from the CCTV you watch like it's injectable and addictive," Vito says.

I guess she is, yes.

"You're deluded." But it's a futile attempt.

"Does she know about the cameras?" Rafe asks.

I pause.

"Do not lie to me," Rafe growls. "I will make Camden pulling out your toenails seem merciful."

"No." Although, as I say it, I wonder, just a bit. Why did she say surveillance? Why was that in her mind? Yes, Morden uses a lot of surveillance and cameras in our work, but still. It's slightly odd.

"But something is happening with you two." Vito lounges against the wall like the Italian he is. He might look identical to Rafe and me but he's always in a sunbeam or striking an elegant pose.

"It's complicated," I mutter.

"We're your brothers," Vito says. "And I'm not putting a spy on you this time. You're going to just tell us without me having to use pliers."

I massage my forehead and consider my options. "If I tell you, will you go away?"

"You're fucking her." Rafe frowns.

"No. I love her." The confession is out before I can stop it, and somehow, it's a relief.

"I called it." Vito grins like a smug bastard, and holds out his hand to Rafe, who is shaking his head.

I glare at my brothers. Technically, they are both very slightly older than me, by seconds, but you wouldn't know it. I have more grey in my hair, more scars, and since they've been married, they're both like stupid teenagers.

"You just cost me a lot of money," Rafe grumbles to me.

I wait for the onslaught of shit about what a morally repugnant person I am, but they seem more preoccupied with settling their bet.

"Would it be suicide or murder if I told Mitcham what his friend has been doing?" Rafe says, almost to himself.

Fear and bile rise in my throat.

"Don't. I'm not…" I can't get the words out.

"You're not what?" asks Vito. "And I think it's assisted suicide," he adds to Rafe.

"I'm not going to do anything about it." It's painful to say, but even worse to acknowledge.

"What? Why?" Rafe says.

"Because I prefer ongoing life."

"We could kill him," Rafe replies calmly. "And yeah. He'll never accept you fucking his daughter."

"I'm not fucking her," I repeat.

"But you'd like to." Vito nods. "We'll just kill him."

"Five minutes ago, you were his ally. I hope you don't pull this bollocks behind my back?" I snipe.

They both look scandalised and hurt, as though I've suggested something really disgusting.

"You're our *brother*," Rafe states. "I'll fuck your shit up every day, but I'm not going to actually murder you."

"Maim, maybe," Vito mutters.

*He's my best friend.* I don't say that to my brothers, but Wes and I are as close as Rafe and Vito.

"Not an option." I stand, hoping to shut down this conversation.

"If you do want to do it yourself, I can—" Vito says with infuriating reasonableness.

"No. No, it's… Okay." I couldn't betray him any more than I could my brothers.

"Just you and your hand, huh?" Rafe nods sceptically. "Alright."

"These are the choices. Death, or wanking." Vito gives me a pitying look.

The girl who holds my heart, or my best friend. Even as she becomes so much more than a lifelong friend. "I'll still have her working for me. She's near, and safe."

That has to be enough.

Maybe I can even teach her one last time. A farewell kiss.

# 10

## MAISIE

Mr Blackwood summons me via email. Just a terse, "Come to my office," at lunchtime the day before the meeting of the Blackwoods and my dad. Unlike the missed calls and messages from my dad—I'm dreading what he might say—I respond to my boss immediately.

Nathan, his assistant, is absent as I walk in, and Sev is at his desk. He's not pretending to work, just sitting back, his suit jacket discarded, and his top button undone. His brows are low. He's so serious, but those blue eyes have a fire of intent that sparks excitement in my belly.

"Mr Blackwood." I shut the door, so we have privacy, and stand before him. We're alone. "You called."

"Thought I'd avoid being shoved in a cupboard tomorrow by seeing you today." He sweeps his gaze down my body.

I tingle everywhere and I can't help but smile. That's as close to an acknowledgement that he wanted to see me as I'm likely to get.

I'll take it.

"What am I teaching you this time, Maisie?" He leans

forward on his elbows, staring at me intently. "I'm at your service. What would you like to do?"

I blink in disbelief. Is he offering?

"Can we go on a date?"

Sev's eyes snap. "A date? What for?"

*To wear you down. To make you think of me as more than your best friend's daughter, and your employee.*

The sexy shows I'm putting on every evening don't seem to be working. Not going to lie, I really thought I'd have had some effect by now. That thing I did with a cucumber was absolutely obscene.

Maybe Sev doesn't like the visual of a girl choking on a vegetable then taking it deep in her pussy.

Am I the weird one here?

Possibly, possibly. Or maybe he has an allergy?

I shrug. "I'd like a date for the same reason as any girl would, I guess? To feel attractive, wanted, and admired. To have a man interested in being with me. To have a man's eyes on me."

I venture further than I should with that last comment, but Sev is glaring—that's the only accurate description—as though I'm asking for unicorn balls for supper.

"You don't feel pretty." It's not quite a question.

I do when I imagine his gaze on my body, but another week has passed without him doing anything, and I'm exhausted.

"No," I whisper. "I feel... Ignored."

The air goes thick as gravy between us.

"And unappreciated?" His expression suggests this conversation is a punishment for him. "In your job?"

I give a tiny nod.

"In your private life?"

"I don't get to have a private life!" I burst out. "My father won't even consider me dating. I tried once and the boy gave up, too scared." Admittedly I was eighteen at the time, and since then it's been only me and my book boyfriends. "I love my books and my job, but it's not the same as a *person*."

I love that Sev sees me, but I need him to see *him* more.

"I just want to go out for a nice dinner and have a man look at me like I'm worth something," I finish pathetically.

Sev's gaze slips from mine, and he puts his head in his hand, massaging his forehead with his fingers, using the sort of pressure that seems the opposite of relaxing.

I'm not sure what to do. He appears even more irritated than usual.

"It's okay." I pin my go-to bright smile onto my face. "It doesn't matter."

"It does matter," he snaps, jerking his head up. "It really fucking does, Maisie. You matter."

I might faint. Should I loosen my corset or something? Where are smelling salts when you need them?

"You're going to get me fucking killed, sweetheart," he mutters under his breath but he's on his feet and around the desk before I can figure out what he means. "Come on."

He grabs my arm and tows me to the door, and then appears to realise what he's doing. He's touching me.

He lets out a frustrated sound as he releases me and shoves the door open.

"Go and print off every document you have about the Parkside development. I'll meet you downstairs in ten minutes."

"But you hate paper and say printing is a waste," I ask, confused.

"I say it's a *fucking* waste, yes, but I do not care how many trees you murder, Maisie. I will poison those fuckers with bleach myself and pulp their green shoots with my heel. Print off a stack of paper—or find one of those towers of dead trees that you like so much—and meet me downstairs. You have nine minutes left."

I'm absolutely speechless, and frozen for a second. My boss is... I mean, perhaps he's finally lost it. The raving about tree death certainly supports that theory.

"Now," he snarls, and I scurry away, my heart pounding. It's only when I reach the elevator, thankfully open, that I look back at him.

He is gazing after me, pulling his hand through his silver-streaked hair, and his blue eyes are electric with intensity.

A shiver goes down my spine as the metal doors close.

I don't have to print much. I grab up piles of technical drawings and plans, and some lengthy reports. The clock ticks down in my head and when Trish from accounts asks what I'm doing, I just pant out, "Documents for Mr Blackwood."

She gives me a sympathetic, if baffled, grimace.

"You're late," he says when I get to the lobby less than ten minutes later, my arms full of a stack of paper almost a foot high.

He lifts the documents from me and turns without another word. I follow him out to a car, and I think my brain breaks when we pull up outside a restaurant.

I peek up at him curiously.

"My favourite Italian restaurant. Yes, even I have to eat," he replies to my unspoken question as he ushers me inside.

"I thought you drank the blood of innocents and avoided garlic," I mutter, "but this smells delicious." There's the scent of garlic, yes, but also salty butter, fresh bread, herbs, and olives. My mouth waters.

"I like both garlic and have an interest in the blood of innocents. I contain multitudes and no, you can't stake me," he says dryly, but there's a spark in his eyes.

A waiter appears with menus and greets Sev like an old friend, leading us to a discreet table at the back. There are red and white tablecloths and paintings of Italian landscapes on the wall. The bistro-style chairs have cushions and Sev slams down the pile of papers so hard that a couple of our fellow diners look around.

"Sorry," I say, giving them an apologetic smile. Sev glares and the one remaining guy who was eying us curiously turns away guiltily.

"She'll have the alfredo," Sev says as the waiter comes to give us menus. "And I'll have a steak, rare." Drinks are dealt with in the same arrogant fashion, with Sev ordering my favourite without any reference to me.

"I'm allergic to dairy, you know," I say when the waiter hustles away.

"No, you're not."

I snort with laughter. He's right, I'm not. And he knows that because I've made creamy pasta alfredo at home, pawing over the online recipe.

"But why did you order that for me?"

It's not as though I expect him to confess his stalking, but there's a frisson between us as he regards me across the table.

This is beginning to feel like our game. Does he suspect that I know? Does he want me to?

"It's the best thing on the menu apart from the steak, and I didn't think that was your taste," he lies smoothly.

"And the drink? That's what all teenagers are drinking, isn't it?"

"I'm twenty-three," I remind him.

"I'm five years out, so shoot me. You're only about ten minutes from being a child, whereas I'm a sixteen-hour trip in an aeroplane, three-hours in a car, then thirty minutes on foot."

"Still know what a young woman likes though, don't you?"

There's really hardly any innuendo in my words, but Sev hears me exactly.

His gaze drops to my lips.

"I know what you *need* Maisie," he replies, so low I barely hear him. "Scatter some of those documents over the table," he directs at normal volume, with a flick of his fingers.

His summer-sky-blue eyes assess my movements as I place an architect's drawing in front of him, and a biodiversity report before me.

"Good girl," he says, and this time his voice is pure sex. It flashes right to my core.

"So what's going on here?" I ask breathlessly.

"That," he points at my stack of papers. "Unnecessary waste of a tree's life is making this a working lunch." There's a beat of silence. "But we both know it's a date."

## 11

## MAISIE

I shake my head and laugh. Even I'm aware this is an unusual way to have a date.

"Now we have our facade of a working lunch in place," he says seriously, "I want you to tell me about yourself."

"What?" You could knock me down with a feather.

"That's what people do on dates, no? They get to know each other. I am here, and you have my whole attention. Talk to me. Tell me anything you like." He leans back, relaxing his body even as his mind is as alert as ever.

"Well, the Parkside development—"

"No," Sev cuts me off. "If that's really the thing your heart desires to tell me, then okay. But it's just a cover, Maisie. This isn't actually a work meeting. It's a date. Tell me something you're passionate about. A hobby? Do you read, perhaps?"

I press my lips together.

He knows I read.

"Tell me what you do in the evenings when you're not going on dates."

Dangerous truths shimmer in the air. We're edging too

close to the truth, and I go mute. I can't think of anything that isn't, "I don't dance on tables."

His gaze doesn't waver, and he waits with un-Sev-like patience. He doesn't look away, or glance at the clock. He doesn't even reach for his glass when our drinks arrive.

No, he just looks at me as though I'm the sun and he's a terrifying overgrown Triffid plant-monster who gains energy from my presence, as I flounder and wonder what I should say.

What can I possibly say that would interest a silver fox like Severino Blackwood? Older. Billionaire. Notoriously bad-tempered mafia boss.

Stalker. Orgasm giver.

I can't figure out what to say for around eleven-and-a-half million years, or probably a minute.

Sev, meanwhile, seems happier by the second. He relaxes. The scowl that I thought was chiselled into his brow melts away. And I swear... Is he smiling? Just the tiniest upturn of his generous mouth. A secret little smile that I feel is only for me.

Is this how he looks when he watches me on those cameras I found in my apartment?

And suddenly, I have my voice. I've been longing to have someone to tell about my opinions on a really popular vampire book series, and Sev is offering to listen.

I tell him. Everything. And he listens with all the appearance of loving this. I'd be incredulous, except that I don't think my boss can act.

Our food arrives, and I talk with my mouth full. Sev eats too, slowly. He barely glances at it, cutting the bloody steak without a care for the proximity of his fingers to a sharp knife. Whenever I pause, he interjects with a question, luring me out.

I wanted to be seen? I wanted a man to pay attention to me? Sev pays attention like there will be a life-or-death test at the end of the meal.

For my mother, I was always the audience for whatever drama was happening to her. I didn't mind it. She wasn't interested in my dull little stories from school when she could tell me about her own troubles. It never occurred to me to question that. And when my mother was ill, everything was about her.

My father is profoundly uninterested in anything I say or do.

I don't know how, but talking about books slides into telling him about myself. I don't even know what Sev says to prompt it, but I tell him about my mother's death, and my father's controlling behaviour when I moved in with him at sixteen.

And he listens without judgement.

"I've been ignoring his calls," I confess, but I don't admit why. My dad threatened to sell me off as a mafia princess to benefit Mitcham, from when I was eighteen onwards. Getting a degree saved me at first, but the reason I got this job is I had to get away. Have some of my own money, so when Dad tried to force me to marry against my wishes, I had options.

Instead, I've fallen in love with his best friend, who is also my boss. I thought this was a crush, and I've told myself it doesn't matter that Sev won't claim me. But it does. I love him.

And the way my dad keeps trying to call and talk to me has my spine prickling cold. I'll have to choose, sooner or later. Escape, freedom, and never see the man I love again. Or stay, and end up married to a London mafia boss of my dad's choosing, and maybe be able to see Sev from afar. Sometimes.

And that might have to be enough. I trail to a halt in my chatter when the waiter comes to collect the plates I'm surprised to discover are empty. I squirm with discomfort that I've said way too much. Bored him. This could be one of my last chances to really spend time with him, and I just wasted it telling him about myself and my fictional companions.

Sev has eaten the salad as well as the steak, and it occurs to me that he is an actual adult, with mature tastes and decision-making that give him a body I suspect from the slight views I've had of his forearms, touching his chest, and sitting on his muscled thighs, is sculpted by discipline and work in the gym.

"She'll have tiramisu, I'll have an espresso," Sev orders.

"What about you?" I ask when the waiter has left again. "Tell me about you, since this is a date." I tingle at that word. My first proper date. Well. Fake date.

"What about me?" Sev shrugs. "There's nothing interesting about me."

Apart from being powerful, gorgeous, and bad-tempered. "I bet there is."

"You want to know about my childhood? How my brothers and I fought our way up through the London mafias? How I covered my scars with tattoos, and there is barely an inch of my chest that isn't inked? How I did things that I regret to gain the power I have?"

His jaw clenches. This is a reminder that Sev isn't tame. He's brutal and powerful and I shouldn't be playing with fire.

"My brother Rafe made it his pet mission to save the school we went to and make it less shit. Vito left for Italy in a thinly-veiled search for some connection to our roots, but ended up doing the same thing Rafe and I did—accumulate power."

His mouth twists. "There's nothing interesting about me. I sabotaged Rafe, and he sometimes responded. I'm richer than either of them, and Morden is more powerful." He heaves a sigh. "But now they're both married and have families on the way, and I just have cold, hard cash."

"You're friends with my dad, too," I'm compelled to point out. "And you do good things in Morden. You're a good boss."

He pins me with a look of such intense hunger it takes my breath away.

"I am neither a good friend to your father, nor a good boss. I am not a good man, Maisie, and it would be better for you to remember that."

"You're a good friend to me," I say impulsively, reaching across the table and taking his hand. Paper creases beneath my elbow and Sev blinks in shock.

"I'm definitely not your friend, Miss Matthews. Do not mistake me." The words are harsh, but for almost the first time in this meal so far, he turns away. He can't look me in the eyes as he lies to me, I realise.

We are friends. More than friends, too. He's my boss, my forbidden lover, my stalker. My teacher.

But he is also my friend.

And he doesn't let my hand go. No, he traps it beneath his, like a cat that has caught a bird that it shouldn't have, and cannot eat, but must keep and play with all the same.

We're so close. I can almost taste the truth between us. He's as lonely as I am. He wants a family like his brothers have, and I crave that too. We've worked together for two years, and I know this man's stormy moods better than the familiar London skyline out of my office window.

"Sir."

My head snaps up and I jerk my hand back guiltily, but Sev holds on, and my heart springs into my throat like a bouncing baby animal.

"Espresso and tiramisu, enjoy." The waiter sets the cream, coffee, and chocolate dessert down in front of me, and a tiny cup of coffee in front of Sev, then his gaze snags on our joined hands for a beat. I bite my lip. But Sev isn't letting up. He doesn't let me escape, and the waiter retreats wordlessly.

And when Sev calmly lifts his coffee to his lips as though this is what we do now. Like he only has one hand available, and so do I, and who needs two hands? Overrated.

"Eat," he orders when I just sit there in shock. Because this isn't normal for my boss.

I pick up my spoon and dig into the layered dessert. It explodes on my tongue, but I can't really taste how delicious it is. How decadent.

Because in the silence, Sev begins to stroke his thumb over the back of my hand, gentle and insistent, and my insides melt.

"I guess the story I should tell you is something fun, rather than try to scare you. When we were fifteen, Rafe, Vito, and I made some money—I won't say how, that's less savoury—and we decided to celebrate. Vito was just beginning to embrace our Italian heritage. So he insisted we go to a chain Italian restaurant because we're teenagers who didn't realise that is about as similar to Italian food as I am to a gorilla."

"A silverback gorilla..." He kind of is like that.

A smile ghosts over his face. "Indeed. So Vito says this is educational, and he orders everything on the menu."

I giggle. "Seriously?"

Sev nods, a nostalgic softness in his eyes as he says, "He was an idiot. This food starts piling up. They wouldn't give us anything without payment, so he threw notes on the floor like a five-year-old amped up on sugar in charge of a crime syndicate... Which is pretty much what we were, even then."

I'm entranced. This is Sev as I've never seen him.

"Vito hates half of it. His mouth twists every time he eats an olive because they're so salty and oily. And there are pizzas for miles. Forty, maybe? I forget. And he insists we're going to all try everything, and we'll eat the lot."

"Oh noo... Were you sick?"

Sev gives me a pitying look. "More than once. All of us. I couldn't even look at Italian food for about two years."

Then he's telling me about their first tattoos, and the time Rafe's got infected and when they eventually dragged him to the doctor the dragon looked like a goat, and it had to be inked over and begun again. And when Sev wore too much aftershave, started a fight when Vito called him on it, and they had to sleep in the corridor for a week because the bottle broke and spilt into the carpet of their joint bedroom.

There are other stories, I know. The ones he alluded to. Dark things that happened to him and his triplet brothers, but he doesn't tell me those, and my heart is so light.

He's revealing to me parts of himself I could never have imagined, and from the way he shakes his head, and looks into my eyes, I'm certain he hasn't told anyone this for years. Decades. Possibly ever.

We sit for hours, talking, until the restaurant is empty of lunchtime customers, and the staff are beginning to make subtle hints that he'd like to close up before dinner service. Sev ignores him for a while, but eventually I glance across at him enough that he rolls his eyes and flicks his fingers for the bill.

"Did Mr Blackwood's lady enjoy her meal?" the waiter asks me, placing two little wrapped squares of chocolate beside my plate.

"I'm not his lady," I blurt out, then immediately regret it when Sev's expression darkens. Shit. "I mean, I'm his..." Nothing. I'm just a girl he watches but won't do anything about. I'm beginning to doubt my sanity. "He's my boss."

There's an awkward silence as he slides a sceptical glance to Sev, who has returned to his statue mode.

"Thank you." The waiter turns to go, and my cheeks heat. He must think... God knows what he imagines is going on.

Sev pays without meeting my eyes.

I've totally messed up his favourite restaurant for him.

"Sorry," I whisper when we're in the car on the way back to the office.

"What?" he snaps.

"They know." I grasp around for the right words. "About... Us."

Sev scowls, rubs his forehead, and doesn't reply.

And I realise that maybe there isn't any such thing as us. He might stalk me. He might teach me. I might love him. But I'm just his dirty little secret.

# 12

## SEV

I'm a liar.

I promised not to touch her. I said never again. Then one last time.

But I can't give her up.

It feels even lonelier than usual when Maisie leaves work. I hate that I couldn't find words to make it right when she was upset earlier. I hate that we had to pretend we weren't on a date, and that she denied it. This sneaking around is killing me in ways I didn't expect.

But I can't stop needing her in my life.

I get my phone out and follow the little blinking dot as it tracks all the way to her building, then switch to the cameras in time to see her walk through the door of her apartment. Going into the lounge, she hops onto the sofa, and for a second I'm convinced she glances up and straight into the camera as she smiles tiredly.

It feels like she's smiling at me.

I relax a little as I watch her make dinner, and do some chores. It's a tepid, faded version of spending a long lunch date with her. But it's familiar. It's good enough.

In truth, it's scraps that I'm convincing myself aren't making me famished for the sound of her voice and the feel of her skin on mine.

Today at the restaurant was risky, and tomorrow is a pit of despair because I can't have lunch with her again so soon. I mustn't take her out for lunch every day, as I'd like to. We'd be caught sooner or later, just as we'll be discovered kissing in my office or in a storeroom.

On the one hand I cannot stay away, and on the other I'm betraying my friend. The slight frown on Wes' face when we were in that meeting after I delayed it to eat her pussy returns to me.

If only death weren't so final, I wouldn't mind Wes murdering me for being with his daughter.

I take a deep breath and remind myself, again. He's my friend. I'm so much older than Maisie. This is wrong... But the wrongness is so insubstantial compared to the feelings I have for her.

I need a reminder of why I can't claim her. Why she isn't mine, and never can be.

Picking up the phone, I go call Wes, but as I do, on the screen I see Maisie go to her front door, and pause.

She lets in her father, and gives him a dutiful hug and a smile that though anyone in the world think she's happy, I know better. She's worried.

Hours of working with her, and just as I suspect she sees through my dark moods and grumpy masks, I can see past her bright facade.

I can't hear what they're saying, I can't lip-read, and fuck, I wish I'd set the cameras up with sound.

They go to the kitchen and Maisie makes a cup of tea for Wes. She has to search in the cupboard for different tea bags for him, her cheeks heating.

I don't like this.

Wes might be my best friend, and he's an important ally for Morden, but he's making my girl nervous.

She goes to hand him the mug of tea, and he says something right at that moment and she jerks in shock. Tea splashes over the edge of the mug, and onto her hand.

Like the last time she was hurt, I'm on my feet in a second.

The primal part of my brain is sounding a shrill fire alarm. It's all I can do to not race to Maisie's apartment.

On the screen, Maisie thrusts her hand under running water and clears up the spilt tea as best she can with one hand.

Wes is talking to her, and my frustration with not knowing what's being said mounts with my craving to look after my wounded girl. How bad is the burn?

And what the fuck did Wes say that has her slumping over the sink, her shoulders up around her ears and her head bowed.

They continue to talk, and I'm caught, a fly on a sticky trap. I have to go to her, but I can't just turn up for no reason.

Wes is looking increasingly irritated. Finally, he crosses his arms.

Then I notice Maisie's shoulders. They're vibrating. Lifting up and down. For a moment, I don't understand why. Then she turns and there are tears streaming down her face as she says something to Wes.

Watching her fall off the table is nothing, *nothing* compared to this.

I don't hesitate. I'm out of the office, punching the elevator call button, and swearing.

If Maisie is crying, I'm going to her. There's nothing in

my head but that single, primal need to get to my girl and comfort her. Protect her. Care for her and dry her tears.

Destroy anything that has upset her, even if he's my best friend.

Throwing myself into the nearest car when I reach the basement level, I drive through red lights, and I don't keep the app open and see what she's doing. There's no consideration of stopping.

I love her. She needs me.

The route to her apartment block is familiar, but it has been a long time since I stepped out of the car and used my key to the building. Not since I installed the hidden cameras myself.

I know what apartment is hers. There are raised voices coming from inside, muffled but my heart is thudding out of my chest. I hit the door hard enough to be heard, and pull out my phone to call Maisie. For half a second I think of calling Wes, but there's no need to do either, as within seconds Maisie has wrenched open the door.

"Sev." And although she looks shocked, she doesn't sound surprised. I snatch her into my arms as she falls towards me, her face tear-streaked, her eyes pink.

Pushing her into her oh-so-familiar apartment without a word, I kick the door closed behind us, keeping her tight to me. Fuck, she's so precious.

"Sev?" Wes screws up his face in disbelief. "What are you doing here?"

"What did you do to make her *fucking cry*?" I shoot back, because that's the only thing that matters right now.

"It's family business." He bristles, confused as a tiger meeting a polar bear.

"What are you doing?" Fury burns through my blood.

Wes sets his jaw stubbornly, in an expression I recognise from our years of friendship. "I don't ask you to reveal Morden secrets, you shouldn't expect me to tell you Mitcham's—"

"He wants me to marry the kingpin of Waltham," Maisie says, her voice muffled by being face-first in my shirt and still sobbing.

"No." That's not happening.

"It's already done," he states. "It's just a marriage of convenience."

"No." Louder this time.

"Look, he's about the same age as Maisie." He scowls. "She can't be the Mitcham princess working for Morden forever. This is a decent match. He's alright."

"He's an arsehole." And that's true. He's better than the little prick Kane Anderson killed, but no one could be good enough for Maisie.

"It's not like I'm threatening to send her to the Essex virginity auctions," Wes says frustratedly. "But I do demand that my daughter do something to help Mitcham, and that means marrying for advantage and alliance."

"If anyone is going to marry Maisie, it's me."

"Really?" Maisie looks up at me, her eyes wide with amazement.

"You hate Waltham that much?" Wes spits. "They're not that bad to make my daughter marry a man twice her age."

Then he seems to finally notice that Maisie is clinging to me like a baby koala. "What's going on?" His tone goes icy. "Take your hands off my daughter."

"No." That's not an option. She clutches at me harder, and my arms take up the slack. I can't let her go. Not now, not ever.

"She's my daughter, you bastard!" He takes me by the

lapels, and I let him. "She's twenty years younger than you! You were fucking and fighting when she was in nappies!"

"Dad, stop it!" Maisie lets go of me to reach for Wes, but he's not listening to or looking at her.

"Have you been screwing her?"

"She's an adult," I say at the same time as Maisie says, "So what if he has?"

That's not the denial he wanted, and it's stupid, because it hasn't gone that far. But I want it to.

I'm done with sneaking around. I'm finished with lies, and there won't be any more pretending that this girl isn't the most important thing in the world to me.

"I love your daughter and I'm going to marry her."

Wes shakes me, letting out a howl of anger and frustration. I see his punch coming with easily enough time to move, but I don't. I let him have this, and pain explodes through my jaw.

I deserve it.

"Sev!" Maisie cries in distress.

"I trusted you to look after her!" he yells, pulling out a gun, and cocks the safety.

I go still, my mind calm and blank.

"Dad, no!" Maisie screams.

I knew this was possible. He meant what he said about killing any man who touched his daughter, and drawing my own weapon isn't an option. I promised I'd stay away from her, and I broke my word.

And I don't regret it. If I die, I die honestly, and protecting the girl I love.

"What happened, Maisie?" Wes demands, not looking away from me, the gun unwavering. He cares about her, in his own haphazard way. "He took advantage of you. Tell me exactly what he—"

"I love him," she screeches in panic.

She loves me? Glancing across to her, it's like taking off sunglasses. I'm blinded by the light of her. That's... Insane. Too much.

"I love you too, sweetheart," I say softly, and at least she knows. I came for her when she was hurting, and I love her too much to care if the consequences are fatal for me.

"He's old enough to be your father—" Wes chokes.

"But he's not my father, and he didn't take advantage. And it's..." She looks up at me, and my heart does that amateur gymnastics thing that it took up when we first met. "Love. It's right. And I'm not marrying anyone but Sev."

I hold out my hand and hope and confidence flare in her eyes as hers interlocks. Squeezing her fingers, I'm struck again by how small she is. How precious.

There's a tense silence.

Wes' hand begins to shake. "When did this start?" he grits out, but doesn't lower his gun.

That's a question I don't want to answer.

"How long has this been going on?" he insists.

"I asked him to kiss me a couple of weeks ago," Maisie says, and it's the perfect combination of honesty and bare-faced lie of omission.

"A few weeks?!" he roars.

I nod, not trusting myself to speak. I can lie, but Wes is still my best friend.

The gun goes off so suddenly, for a second I think he's shot me. But I don't fall, so I swing around to check on Maisie. Then Wes has dropped his arms, and I realise there's a hole in the wall two inches to the side of my head.

I let out a shaky breath. That wasn't him missing. He's decided to let me live.

Wes spins abruptly, holstering his gun, then sweeps his

hands through his black hair, just like his daughter's, and lets out a yell of frustration.

None of us move.

"I hate this," he mutters. "I knew it. I *knew* something was up between you two."

Maisie reaches out with her free hand. I give her a warning squeeze, but I think his violence has burnt its hottest.

Probably.

"Dad..."

"Do not 'Dad' me," he snaps. "You two are awful, shitty—"

"Wes," I interrupt with a threat in my tone. There's only so much I'll take, and the amount is zero for Maisie. I won't allow him to be rude to her, mortal threats to my life or not.

"Don't. You're lucky to be alive." He plants his hands on his hips and looks over his shoulder, then away again, as though the sight of us together, our hands linked, is more than he can deal with.

"This is happening with or without your approval," I state clearly. If I have to steal Maisie away and break ties with my best friend, well. So be it.

Today has reorientated my priorities in a way that makes me wonder why this realisation took me so long.

"I can't believe I didn't see it sooner," he says, almost to himself. "You sneaky shitheads."

Maisie and I exchange a tentative look of hope.

"I'm sorry, Dad," Maisie begins, "But—"

"I know, I know, give me a minute you arseholes," Wes grumbles, bowing his head as though at the funeral of good sense and taste, and really mourning their loss.

I feel Maisie's excitement buzzing and when I brush my

thumb over hers and she pushes her little fingertips into my knuckles, it's a promise.

"You'll formalise the alliance with Mitcham," he says, his back still to us.

"Of course, how much were you thinking of?" I've built a fortune once, doing it a second time would be a small price for Maisie.

Wes huffs. "I don't need your money, you prick. You'll take my side when Westminster wants to short-change everyone south of the river, and you'll *marry*."

"I'm no more fond of being fleeced than you are, and a better ally than Waltham," I say to Wes, not quite daring to look at Maisie even as I bring our joined hands to my lips and kiss the back of her hand. "I'll ask your daughter about the second thing. I hope she'll say yes."

Maisie blinks, then nods eagerly.

"In return I'll pay you for that laundering you do for me," Wes says between gritted teeth.

"Good of you." I'm grinning, because I'm winning all the way here. I'm stupidly, improbably happy.

"Don't hurt her." Wes turns and faces me down.

"I won't."

"If you break her heart, I will personally skin you alive, then dip you in acid." Right now, Wes is not my friend. He's not a mafia boss. He's a protective father. "Be good to her. Keep her safe."

"Dad!" Maisie protests.

"I will treat her like the princess she is, but not because of any threat from you," I reply with the simple truth.

Wes narrows his eyes.

"I'll love and spoil her as she deserves because doing anything that harmed Maisie would be far more painful than your torture."

"Fine." Wes grimaces, but doesn't enlarge on that.

"You don't mind?" Maisie checks.

"I absolutely do mind." His expression softens as he looks at his daughter. "But I won't kill him since you seem to *like* him."

"Good." I touch my cheek, which is sore and probably going to bruise, but thankfully not that bad. Wes is my friend, it seems, even when he's murderous, and didn't hit me as hard as he could have.

"I love him," Maisie says again, and my heart does a new move. Olympic-winning gymnast, my stupid heart. Missed its calling beating in my chest all day.

Wes huffs, but he holds out open arms. Maisie goes to him, and I let her. My future wife hugs my best friend, her father, and my future father-in-law.

I wait patiently as Maisie says she's not a little girl anymore, and Wes grouches that she's always his little girl. Eventually, Maisie draws back.

"Come on." I pull her to my side. "Leave your dad to get over the shock he's going to be a grandfather sooner rather than later."

Wes growls.

It's just the truth. "There's something I want to show you."

## 13

## SEV

"Where are we going?" Maisie asks as I reach over and drag the seat belt over her. Keeping her safe wasn't just words to me. She's pink-eyed and rumpled, and has never looked so perfect in her life.

"I thought you'd like to go to my place," I say as I turn the car onto the road. "To take a look."

"What do you mean?" She looks me up and down, a little suspicious.

"It's only fair." I shrug. It's a confession, of sorts.

She laughs then, and nods, and it's like the tension of the scene with her dad washes away. "An invitation into the lair of the beast. Who could resist?"

I drive more carefully than I did on the way to her apartment. I'm fine with risking my life, but not hers. Then she's walking in the door of my penthouse, and nerves I've never known I had are buzzing like flies.

I put my hands in my pockets and watch her with an uneasy sensation in my stomach. It's stark and plain, a world away from her chaotic style. I bite my lip to avoid saying she could change that painting for another when she pauses by a Rothko, or get a different sofa when she tests the cushions for bounciness. She examines my space almost in silence, just casting me looks over her shoulder when she discovers something of interest.

She snoops through my fridge and examines the vegetables quizzically.

"I like to cook," I admit, and she shakes her head and laughs.

In one of the cupboards, she finds my cupcake stash.

"Raspberry," she notes, a little surprised.

"I've got a bit of a taste for them," I say, and she smiles that infinite smile.

It takes a while before she gets to my bedroom. It's very plain, and I almost apologise for it. The white sheets. The empty walls. It's not like hers with its multi-coloured throws and soft cushions. But Maisie doesn't seem to mind.

"So, where shall I set up the cameras?" She bounces on the bed, bright eyes looking up at me.

She's mine. She's really, honestly mine. I don't think it sinks in until that moment, with her question stripping away all pretence between us.

"Here," I say, and offer her my hand. She takes it, trusting me, and that's a special gift. I pull her to her feet and guide her to the dressing room that the interior designer said was absolutely necessary, and I've never found a use for. Until now.

I open the door, and she glances in then back in surprise.

It's a room entirely covered in mirrors, floor to ceiling. Her gaze steady on me in the reflection, she steps into the mirrored room, and I smile at the way there's Maisie surrounding me. Perfect.

As I shut us in, her eyes widen.

"I don't think I've ever seen you smile before," she says wonderingly.

"You'll get used to it." I step right up to her. "Time for honesty, sweetheart." I slide my hand around her neck and up her jaw with my thumb.

"Yes." It's a cross between a whimper and a sigh.

"You like me watching you, don't you?" This is throwing all my chips on the table in one reckless bet.

I stroke my palm down her throat as she pauses, and my cock throbs. I want to own her, body and soul, and it's so close I can almost taste it. "And you teased me, didn't you? Once you found out that I was watching."

She presses into my hold and there's excitement in her brown eyes. "It worked."

"Perfectly," I agree. "But you're going to regret goading a monster, Maisie."

"How long have you been watching me?" She licks her lips.

"You know."

"I don't!" she protests, but when I draw closer again, pinning her hips with mine, she gasps and writhes and pleasure surges up my cock where we're pressed together.

I tip her chin with my finger, so she has to look at me.

"Since the beginning. Since we first met at that excuse for a party." I think diving off a cliff without a parachute would be less scary than this. But I've been a coward. I've been watching Maisie from a distance for far too long. "Now what do you want to learn in today's lesson?"

"You. I only want you," she breathes, melting into me. She's so soft. "That's all I ever wanted."

The satisfaction and relief are a jolt of adrenaline.

"Maisie, I can't live without you." I turn her so her back is to my chest, and shift her so we're back in the middle of the room. Holding her against my erection, I roll my hips, so it grinds into the small of her back and she whimpers. "You're *mine*." I gather her hair in my fist, keeping my other arm tight around her waist. "Say it."

"I'm yours," she whispers, and hearing her makes this real in a way I didn't know I needed.

The beast inside me purrs. "I want more than is reasonable, Maisie. I crave your heart, and soul. I need every secret, and every thought."

I tug her hair to pull her head to the side, and kiss down her neck. She smells like raspberries and cream, and I inhale her. I'm addicted.

"And I want to breed you, sweetheart. Put a baby in here." I press on her soft belly.

"Your baby?" Her brown eyes sparkle in the mirror, full of hope.

"Our baby. Mine. Yours. A family."

Her smile is all the answer I need. There are all these mirrors showing Maisie from every angle, but what I most desire is to see her looking back at me.

I could live in this room with her. We might never leave.

"Give me something to watch, princess." I shift to release her enough that she can move, and when our gazes meet again, she's flushed.

Her hands fall to her trousers, and I wait with bated breath as she undoes the buttons. I groan as she pushes her knickers off at the same time, and steps out of her shoes.

"You're more beautiful in person than I could ever have believed when I was watching you on camera," I murmur.

Maisie gives me a sweet smile and peels her top over her head slowly, gradually showing her belly, then the underside of her breasts, then her nipples. Her hair falls as the top comes off altogether and the creamy soft skin of her back is revealed, the perfect contrast to her dark hair. I breathe out in awe.

"Did you see these on your cameras, Mr Blackwood?" She cups her naked, berry-topped breast and gazes up at me.

"Not like this." Not from a dozen different angles. Not when she's so gloriously here, vivid and warm and mine.

"Did you touch yourself as you watched me?" She smooths her hands over her breasts.

She's so hot, the fire down my spine nearly incapacitates me.

"You know I did, Maisie. I blew my load night after night watching you. I imagined your face as I jerked myself off, every time," I rasp.

Her fingers drift to her nipples, rolling them, and my mouth waters with the desire to suck them. I will. I promise myself silently.

"Do it. Show me." The challenge in her expression is so confident, I love it.

"The next time I come it's going to be buried deep inside your tight, hot little cunt," I reply, but I reach for my belt all the same, and keep looking into her face as I release my cock.

Stroking it, slow and deliberate, I lazily trail my gaze over her breasts in the mirror, then return to her eyes. Always back to her pretty face.

"Can you see how hard you make me? How much I want you? You give sunsets self-doubt, Maisie, you're that beautiful. You make kittens feel inadequate because you're so soft and cute."

She huffs a laugh, but she's blushing and pleased. "What does that make you?"

"A greedy, covetous monster who will do anything to

have you," I confess brokenly. "Just a man, stalking a girl half his age, asking her to be mine. And taking you if you don't say 'no' quickly enough."

"You didn't ask, Sev."

I hate that she's right. I reach around her and grab her breast, cupping it and squeezing her nipple until she gasps and wiggles against me.

"You're the daughter of my friend, Maisie. This is dirty. You shouldn't want a man twice your age. When you turned up at my company, sweet and twenty-one, I betrayed that trust. I moved you into an apartment I'd put cameras in, and jerked off watching your young, virgin body on the screen." I roll my length against her arse with each word.

"Fuck, you feel even better than I imagined all those nights. You're fresh, forbidden raspberries and cream. Would you like to know what I dreamed of as I made myself come for you, Maisie?"

"Me, on my knees, and you ramming your cock into my throat?" she whispers.

"And I thought it wasn't possible for me to be any harder." I drift my hand down her body, over her belly, then down. "Look at that," I growl. "Look."

We both regard my big hand covering her mound. So lewd and wrong, and yet so right.

Going further, I touch a flood of her arousal. I slide one finger into her folds and over her clit, and she bucks and cries out.

"I will do everything I've been thinking of for two years. But first and foremost, you're going to come on my fingers. Then my cock. Then my face."

It's almost too easy to push my fingers into her tight wet little body, and she practically collapses in my arms as I begin to rub her, keeping up a relentless rhythm on her virgin hole and teasing her nipples too. One, then the other, pinching and rolling them.

She makes needy little sounds as I stroke her clit, and my cock is bursting with the need to fuck her. But I don't. Not yet. I keep going with this torture for us both.

"I fantasised about burying my cock in your pussy, thrusting into you, and coming deep inside you, right against your womb to breed you with a baby so we're a family, together."

"I want that." She gasps as I circle her clit harder. "Sev, please. I want everything."

"I know, I know," I soothe her. "We'll do that after you come for me like the good girl you are."

She begins to sob as the sensations intensify. As I get more impatient to feel her break for me.

"I watched you touch yourself, a perfect good girl, teasing her stalker, and even more than I longed to push you onto your back and feast on your delicious cunt until you scream, I wanted this."

I look down at her, rather than in the mirror.

Seeing my hands on her makes this all the more real, and pleasurable. And I think it does for Maisie too, as she has one hand in my hair and the other on my thigh. My undone trousers have left my cock sticking out, but it's forgotten by both of us as her pussy tightens on my fingers. She's close.

"I've craved holding you and feeling you quake as you come. So do it, Maisie."

She keens, so close.

"Let me feel it." Then our eyes meet in the mirror. "I love you. Come for me."

She clamps onto my fingers and her bliss reverberates through me as well, from my hands to my heart, shaking my core. But she doesn't shut her eyes, or look away. She's as compelled as I am.

I catch her as her knees give way and hold her to me.

She's barely able to stay on her feet as I lift her in my arms, bridal style.

"What?" she says vaguely, as I leave the dressing room behind and carry her to my bed.

"This is where I would watch you from, sweetheart. Where I stroked my cock night after night, thinking of you for two long, lonely years." I toss her onto the bed, and she squeals as she bounces. I'm on her immediately, covering her with my body. "This is where it began, this is where it ends, and begins anew."

## 14

## MAISIE

He kisses me like there's nothing else he desires. As though kissing is an end in itself, and his cock isn't rock-solid against me.

His lips on mine are soft and patient, coaxing and tender, just as they were when he taught me how to kiss.

Below the waist it's a different story.

We're grinding against each other. Or rather, he's bearing down on me, and I'm writhing helplessly, trying to get closer. I have an empty feeling in my lower belly. The ache is absurd, but no less intense for that. It's as though my body recognises that we belong together, and every second we're not joined, the need increases.

His clothes are deliciously rough on my bare skin, and my fingers grip his hair. That hair I've looked at so many times over the years since he's been my boss. And he wanted me all that time, just as I did him. It's almost too good to be true.

My hands slide down, and I'm gripping his neck as he rubs his cock between my legs where I'm slick and desperate. Then I'm hampered in my exploration by his shirt collar.

"Sev," I gasp. "Take it off." It's hard to get the words out between his lips on mine, but I tilt my jaw, and he shifts to rasping his stubbled chin over my neck and I moan.

I had no idea I was sensitive there. It feels so good, I almost lose my grip on what I was asking, because Sev isn't listening, he's devouring me.

"Later," he mutters.

"Now." He's big, and I'm trapped beneath him, but I try to get at his shirt first, attempting to undo his buttons.

"Have to see you," I pant. My brain isn't working fully. Half my brain cells are between my legs and the other half intent on seeing Sev's body.

He groans. "Such a demanding little thing, aren't you?" He presses his lips to my throat. "I don't think I can, Maisie. I can't move even an inch from you."

"I have to see and feel you. All of you. Please," I beg.

And that's what causes my huge, scary, determined man to stop. He levers himself up, and his blue eyes are dark, the pupils massive as he gazes down at me. His hair is messy where I've been stroking it, and he looks wild. Feral.

"The things you do to me, Maisie." Then he rears up onto his knees, grabs his shirt in both hands and rips it open. Buttons ping and fabric tears, and I squeak in shock.

He's bare to the waist.

My mouth falls open. Sev is everything I dreamed he could be. His chest is muscled, with defined pectorals and abs, and a smattering of dark hair that makes a discontinuous "T" shape, leading downwards, and that definition of muscles at his waist that makes a "V".

He's covered with tattoos. There isn't an inch of his

torso and arms that isn't inked, all the way up to his neck. There are religious symbols covering his arms. Over one shoulder is a lion, eyes staring right into me. It's surrounded by foliage, but native English leaves and flowers, not tropical ones. In the centre of his chest, there's a large "M".

"M for Morden," I say, tracing my finger over the letter, and he huffs.

"Guess again." His eyes crinkle with mirth. "I had that done only two years ago."

I shake my head, not understanding.

"My sweetheart," he says fondly. "M for Maisie."

That steals my breath, and I stare in disbelief. "You got a tattoo for me?"

"You may have noticed," his tone is wry, "I am a little obsessed."

A grin spreads across my face. He is amazing.

"What about the others?" I reach up to indicate his crescent, a cross, a six-pointed star, and the lion.

"Those really are Morden," he replies with an edge of impatience. "Have you looked your fill? I have things I want to do to you."

"For now." Later I want to examine every line on his body.

He shucks off his already-opened trousers and underwear. "Good girl. Because I'm going to have you. I'm going to claim you so thoroughly you'll never have any question about who you belong to again. I'll ruin you for any other man, because who owns you?"

"You do." I love his possessiveness.

"Damn right." He falls forward into my arms and as I stroke his shoulders in awe—his skin is softer than I could ever have imagined—he grasps my chin and holds my gaze.

"For two years you've held my heart. I've thought of you every day, Maisie."

He dips his head, and his mouth finds my breast and without hesitation he's licking and grazing his teeth over the sensitive tip and I'm writhing, the pleasure a lightning strike. I gush with wet heat between my legs as he moves to my other breast, treating it the same and bringing his hand to pinch the first, the cool of his saliva heightening my arousal as he rolls my nipple in his fingers.

"You've had me on a leash, and you didn't even know."

"Because you didn't tell me!" I protest but my voice dies off as he sucks my nipple into his mouth. My hips are moving of their own accord, and I'm vaguely aware I wanted to touch him, but he's got me brainless.

A hard tug on my flesh, and I can't help it, I cry out. I wrap my legs around him, desperate to get more. My clit flares with bliss as I manage to catch it on the length of his erection.

"You were a little tease though, weren't you?" He growls and settles over me again, face to face. "You wanted your daddy's best friend, and you taunted him with this tight, pretty body of yours."

He notches the head of his cock between my legs, and I moan as where he's hard meets where I'm soft and wet. "I'll go slow for you, Maisie. But now you'll take your stalker's cock like a good girl. No crying at how big it is when it hurts, because I promise when you get used to my size you'll love it. Beg for it."

"I might beg before then," I admit, rolling my hips.

He makes a rough, dark sound from the back of his throat.

"You're so wet. You're going to feel like heaven, aren't you?"

"I hope so." There's a pinprick of uncertainty. I'm a virgin, for all my seduction of Sev. And he's a man twice my age, who could find me insufficient to his desires.

"No hope required. You're mine. You were made to fit the gap in my heart, and to have a space here," he pushes against my entrance, and I gasp as a pinch of pain strikes through me. "For me."

## 15

## MAISIE

I hold his gaze, losing myself in his blue eyes that are full of love and understanding as he rips me open. Slowly, so slowly, making soothing noises as he stretches me, creating the place inside me that he says is there. And he's right. It is there.

All the same, it hurts, and I whine.

"You're doing so well," he murmurs.

"You're too big."

"I know, I know." He strokes my cheek. "And you're unimaginably tight, Maisie. But trust me. Wait, and trust me."

So I do. I bite my lip at the spike of pain as he pushes further in, until suddenly something in me releases, and he's all the way in, so deep it makes me gasp and clutch him.

Sev is breathing heavily, his forehead pressed to mine, and he groans like this is torment.

Meanwhile, it feels like I'm finally right. Home.

"Are you okay?" I murmur.

Sev gives a cynical chuckle, but it's broken. He kisses me hard. "I am not okay. I am ruined. I am destroyed. I am hanging onto my sanity by a thread because the way your hot wet tight little sheath grips me is going to murder me with your sheer perfection."

Laughter bursts from my chest because that's such a Sev thing to say, and he sounds so aggrieved.

"And now, to add insult to injury, my little pussy assassin is laughing at me."

"Assassin pussy," I point out. "I'm not killing cats, I'm killing you with a—"

He lets out a feral growl and thrusts his hips, withdrawing and slamming back into me hard. It stops me mid-word and forces an undignified sound from my throat. Something between a wail and a grunt.

"That's more like it," he croons, and does it again. "I thought you'd need my cock in that sweet, smart mouth to silence you, but no."

He sets up a slow but firm rhythm, sending a shower of pleasurable sparks over me each time. It's the best thing I've ever felt. A unique magic of him so close. Inside me.

"I'm glad to see that my cock buried in this tucking stunning pussy shuts you up for once." He grips my hair tight and tugs, and that heightens every sensation.

I'm panting as Sev kisses me again, and it's a sloppy, wet kiss of tongues and passion as he holds my head in place as he fucks me. I kiss him back, and hold on as best I can.

"You're being such a good girl for me. Can you do more?"

"Mm! Yes," I whimper.

"Lift your legs, and spread them wider," he says roughly. "It'll feel even better for both of us, with me deeper inside you."

More joined? Yes. Definitely.

I'm not quick enough for Sev, of course. My impatient

man. He grasps my knee and guides it up and out, and on the next thrust he's right. I grip the back of his neck. The pain is a far-off memory and all I feel is pleasure at the fullness of him inside me.

Impossibly, it's even better, spiralling the pleasurable tension where we're joined and the little nub above.

"Yes. Like that, Maisie," he grits out between thrusts. "You feel... There are no words. Tight and wet and mine. Pinch your nipples for me." He releases my knee, and I keep it high for him as he grabs my hand from his head and brings it to my breast, his covering it. "I'm going to stroke your clit, sweetheart, but you have to roll your nipple between your fingers for me like a good girl until you scream and come on my cock. Clench me hard as you come and if you're very good, after you've come twice more, I'll breed you."

I can't do anything but obey, and the second my fingers touch my nipple, it amplifies the pleasure. Then Sev crams his hand between us, not letting up the relentless pace of his hips against mine and his perfect cock into me—I now concede it's not too big—it only takes a touch and it's the push I need. I come in a shower of white sparks radiating out from his fingers and his cock.

I think I scream. I definitely break apart in the best way, as Sev kisses and hushes me through it all.

When my brain is functioning again and the pleasure has subsided to just ripples and a happy weakness in my legs, I discover Sev has slowed his pace of sliding his body into mine almost to a stop. He's just luxuriating in being together, as though it's an indulgence.

But he's solid as a rock inside me.

# 16

## SEV

I'm so happy, this is surely illegal. Immoral. Wrong.

But it's not. I have claimed my woman, and my best friend has given his grudging approval.

"I love you and will make up for all our lost time, sweetheart." I've stopped moving, just focusing on the exquisite sensation of her pleasure around my cock, and the look on her face. The joy of her beneath me and there being no need to be furtive is indescribable. There's nothing to hide. Not my love for her, or the fact I'm obsessed. I flex my hips as she's still recovering from her orgasm.

I smile as I shift, without slipping out of her, and settle onto my heels, her sweet little arse and lower back on my thighs and her legs splayed out on either side of my waist. Her shoulders are still on the bed, that inky black hair stark on the sheets.

I love it.

She lets out a whimper of pleasure as I lift one of her legs to my shoulder, and kiss her ankle. The other leg falls out, and the way she's spread wide is so fucking sexy.

"Use me," she whispers, her eyes flickering open and

looking right at me. "Use my body to make yourself feel good."

"What?" My brain stutters, even as I instinctively begin to move into her. The view of her is better than I've ever imagined. My cock disappearing into her wet entrance, glistening and slick. She's pink and a little bit swollen. The cream we're making together as I thrust into her is pink with her virgin blood, and the satisfaction I feel that I tore into her is savage.

"I want to be everything you need." She gazes up at me with trusting, sparkling eyes. Happy. "It makes me hot to think of being the one you turn to. Being enough for you."

"Enough?" I stop. I have no idea how, since my cock is screaming at me. But that word won't do. "You're not merely enough for me, sweetheart."

Bringing one hand to her clit again, I circle it gently, testing her for it being too soon. Her gasp says it's not. I stare down into her eyes, and my heart could burst with how much I love her. "You are exactly right for me in every way. You could only be perfect. My good girl." I thrust deep. "My best girl."

"Yes. Sev, please. Use me." She grips the bedding.

I take her at her word, working her on my cock. I press the heel of my hand down onto the place in her belly where she's speared and filled by me, feeling her from both sides, my hand and my cock, while I rub her clit.

"You're so slick and tight, you feel like heaven. Being such a good girl for me." I thrust harder, and then I can't help it. I'm speeding up.

But I'm intent on her pleasure, too, so even as my balls tighten, and the pressure spirals at the base of my spine, I'm watching for the place that makes her shudder and moan.

And yes, I'm using her. I lift her hips to get her onto my cock faster and deeper.

"Come, Maisie. I can't hold on and I need to fill you up and make you pregnant."

Her cheeks go pink, and she whines, almost lifting herself off the bed from her tense forearms.

"I'll use you as my precious, perfect sex toy, filling you up over and over until my seed is permanently sliding down your thighs. I'm going to fuck my baby into you."

She's sobbing now, just needing that spark to tip her over.

"Milk it out of me," I say hoarsely. "If you want it, take it, sweetheart. Take it." I slam into her, my hands grasping. "I love you."

She clenches around me, and I feel her orgasm before I hear her choked scream and see her shake with the intensity of it. And this time, I can't hold on. One more stroke into her lush, beautiful body, and then I come.

I've never felt anything like it. My balls pull up as jet after jet wracks through me and into her. It's an explosion of pleasure. I've lost control of myself. I roar. This girl is mine, and marking her by coming inside her is a primal satisfaction.

I'm broken. Mind, body, both destroyed. My heart is hers, given entirely, with every part of myself. As I promised, I filled her up.

But I'm not hollow. I'm full too.

Somehow, I manage to lie down and have her in my arms, careless of how messy we both are. My hands are sticky from her juices, and between her thighs and all over and around my cock is soaked. But when I lie on my side and press my forehead to hers, my chest is overflowing with love. It might be my love for her, or hers for me, I don't have a clue.

All I know is that when I kiss her, she whispers, "I love you," and I say the same thing back to her, and that is all that matters, and will ever matter.

I can't move, and neither can she. I think we nap, and when I open my eyes, Maisie is tucked into my chest, and she's awake, tracing her fingers across my skin.

"Did you mean it that you've watched me from when I started working for Morden?" she asks, her lips on the tattoo I got only weeks after we met.

"Yes." I turn and press my lips to the top of her head. "There has been no one else since we met. You're everything, and you always will be. I could no more think of loving another woman than a deep-sea fish could leave the ocean. It would be death. It would be throwing away all the things that nourish me, let me breathe, and give me joy."

"Ohh." She sighs happily.

"You're mine, Maisie. I meant that. You're mine, and I'm yours."

# EPILOGUE
## MAISIE

7 YEARS LATER

He's still a stalker, my husband.

I'm with the kids in the playroom, on my hands and knees as we play zoo. I'm a horse. Tommaso is a hippo, Josie is a rabbit—even though her twin Jackie is grumpy that rabbits aren't zoo animals—Jackie is a monkey, and Ginevra is a tiger. We are all crawling around on the floor, except for baby Aldo, who is asleep in his crib on the other side of the room.

He, according to his big sister Josie, is a mouse.

"Arrrr!" Tommaso makes an indistinct noise.

"What was that?" Ginevra asks, coming out of tiger character.

"'Ippo!" Tommaso says delightedly. He is just three, and shakes his head in what I think is supposed to be a hippo action.

"It was a growl, but I'm the tiger, not you," says Ginevra, skirting along the line of peevish and amused.

"I think it sounded like a wolf," says Jackie, distracted for the moment from her critique of Josie's animal choice.

I suppress a giggle. It did sound a bit wolf-ish.

"You're sure you're not a wolf?" Ginevra says kindly.

"'Ippo," Tommaso insists. "Big."

I don't know what it is that sends a tingle down my spine, but my eyes go to the nanny cam I know he has hidden in most of the rooms in the house—the photo frame with the discreet black dot—and wink.

"Big like his father," I say, and I swear I hear Sev's laugh.

"What animal is Daddy?" Ginevra asks.

"He's a silver fox," I reply before I put on my internal filter. I'm by the sofa, so I give up on being on all-fours, and sit back against the cushions.

Jackie scowls. "That's not a real animal."

"Yes, it is," Josie says loyally. The twins both have Sev's blue eyes, and Jackie is just as serious as her father. It's very sweet.

"It's like an arctic fox?" I suggest. "They're white."

The twins consider this carefully, looking at each other with that twin understanding.

"I don't think so," Ginevra declares. "He hasn't only got white hair. He has dark brown and grey hair."

"A fox is too small," Jackie agrees. "Daddy isn't a silver fox."

My lips twitch. "No. Silly of me. What animal do you think he is?"

"What about a silverback gorilla?" rumbles a voice from the doorway, and we all look up.

"Daddy!" All the kids fly to hug Sev, who scoops them up, laughing. I joked once that he could have as many kids as he could carry, and with Ginevra on his back Josie and

Jackie hanging off one arm, Tommaso on the other, and Aldo in his hands, he says he could still manage two more.

They all tell him, in a jumbled way, about the zoo animals they're being and who is best at it.

"There's nothing for it, we need a competition." Sev points at the rug in the middle of the room, then sinks to his knees so he's at the kids' level. More or less. "Everyone on, and doing your best impression of your animal. Mum will judge."

"What do we win?" asks Ginevra, scampering to obey.

"The greatest prize of all, of course," Sev replies.

"Chocolate?" Ginevra chirps hopefully.

"A raspberry cupcake?" I suggest.

"Pfft." Sev shakes his head. "You two. No. Though I do love raspberries and cream. A kiss."

All the kids groan.

It turns out, there's still sneaking around so no one catches us having naughty sexy times together. Just now it's our kids who might see us, not my dad. Both are equally horrified, but children are less murderous.

"A kiss if I win, a cupcake if it's one of you," he concedes. "Alright. Animals in three, two, one, go!"

I burst out laughing at the chaos that ensues. Sev beats his chest in a very passable impression of a gorilla. Tommaso continues with the roar of some description that is supposed to be a hippo. Josie jumps, the perfect little bunny.

But they all bump into each other and it ends up in a big pile of the kids on top of Sev, and him play-fighting and tickling them.

"Alright, I have my winner!" I call when Sev winces as Tommaso's elbow pokes his balls. I'm fond of that part of my husband, and would rather it remained intact.

"Who, who?!" Ginevra clamours.

"The winner is…" I pause. "Everyone! I made enough cupcakes for everyone this morning."

This is met with groans and cheers and a general feeling that this isn't how competitions work, so they'll have to have their own, this time a race down the corridor.

Sev sits down beside me with a grin, sliding his arm over my shoulders as they all rush off.

I rest my head on Sev's shoulder contentedly and he plays with a wisp of my hair.

"The kids will all be out tomorrow," he muses. He isn't telling me anything I don't already know. We both adore our children, but the days when they're with the nanny are good for everyone. "Would you like a day to yourself, or to come into the office with me? Or shall we both have a lazy day?"

"Office. I think we should discuss the Parkside development," I say innocently. Our code, still, after all these years.

Sev reaches across and tips my chin with his forefinger, a smirk making his blue eyes twinkle. "Print out some information. I'll take a look."

# EXTENDED EPILOGUE
## SEV

7 YEARS LATER, THE NEXT DAY

"Mr Blackwood." My wife walks into my office like temptation itself, and I jerk to look up, blinking.

She has a naughty smile playing around her mouth. "I need your help."

"Anything." That's my immediate response to my wife's requests. Or my children's. They're the centre of my life.

But when she says, "Thank you," I narrow my eyes.

That skirt seems very familiar somehow. Her body has changed since she's had children, getting lusher and curvier. This outfit isn't her current style, but equally, it has a vibe I recognise.

She links her hands behind her back and peers across at me from beneath lowered lashes.

"About my job here," she continues. "It means a lot to me."

Then I notice that her smile is a bit sly. "Go on."

"I'll do *anything* to keep this job."

She licks her lips suggestively and my cock swells at the sight. This is a game we've played before.

"Anything?" I enquire, voice rough and low. "I'm your dad's best friend, you know."

"Yes," there's a hitch in her breath.

My cock is absolutely solid now. Part of me wants to just order her to come and sit on my lap with her skirt up immediately, but there's also pleasure in teasing.

"I'm twenty years older than you, Maisie. Don't you find that dirty?" I draw out the last word, sprawling in my chair, my knees apart.

"Yes. You are a lot older, and my dad would kill us if he found out anything was going on." She pauses, then coyly twists a strand of that jet-black hair—hair I've clenched in my fist so many times—in her fingers.

I shove my chair back so she can see the line of my erection in my trousers. Slowly and deliberately, I reach down to my waist.

Her eyes drop to watch me, and her mouth falls open.

"What would you do, my little off-limits girl?" I toy with my belt buckle. "How much do you want to keep your job?"

"I need it," she whispers, but she's staring right at my cock, her gaze so hot it feels like it could scorch right through the fabric over the bulging length.

"How badly?"

She gives a soft whimper and presses her thighs together.

"How filthy are you willing to be?" I rasp as I push the flat of my palm down the ridge of my cock. Pleasure flares through me, but it's Maisie's response that makes me shudder with lust. She whimpers.

"I'll do whatever you want."

I unbuckle my belt slowly, and release my cock one

layer of fabric at a time. The click of the zip is obscene in the quiet of the room.

She's mesmerised by the sight, just as I am by her body. Sometimes we play this scenario another way, and she begins to strip for me as she tells me how she needs her job, or I order her to take off her clothes, and get her to turn around, showing me every breathtaking inch of her.

"My eager little slut," I purr. "Do you want me to push you to your knees, force your jaw open and shove my thick cock between your lips?"

Her hand goes to her throat, and she's striving for a shocked expression, but I know when Maisie is horny. She's been my wife for a long time now.

She attempts a gasp. "Mr Blackwood!"

"It's so big it'll make your eyes water as I make you take it." I grab my cock and stroke it as we talk. I tell her what I mean with my hands. I need to come. "And I'll hold your head as I fuck your mouth, gripping your hair to keep you in place."

My cock is painfully hard, almost purple, it's so swollen now.

"What do you think? Worth it to keep your job?"

She drags her fingertips down, over her collarbones and to the dip of her cleavage that's barely hidden by her top.

I bite back a groan. "Maybe I'll fuck your throat, then pull out and come all over those perky little breasts of yours."

"You wouldn't," she says with faux shock. "Not to your *best friend's innocent daughter*."

I grin. "I would."

Heat sizzles down my spine. I'm going to enjoy this, and I haven't even decided exactly what to do to her. "I'd claim you and defile you. Maybe I'd shoot my big load onto your face."

She opens her eyes wide as though she's never heard of such a thing, never mind licked my come from her lips. My little liar.

"Is that what I'd have to allow you to do to keep my job?"

Her hand drifts to her breast and pinches one nipple.

I chuckle darkly. "Or perhaps I'll bend you over this desk and take you until you plead with me to let you come."

"I'll do anything, Mr Blackwood. Please. Just don't tell my father that you used me like a whore for your own enjoy—"

"Get over here," I snap. Her satisfied little smile that she broke me makes a possessive, dominant growl rise in my chest.

"You are so fucking naughty. Lift your skirt." Her hands shake as she pulls up the silky material, but she hesitates as she gets to the top of her thighs. "Keep going."

"I..." She's blushing, and fuck, I adore this. I adore her.

"Are you wearing any knickers, you bad girl?"

"No," she confesses in a whisper.

I can't breathe. She was walking around without any underwear, with that short skirt on? I have to hold onto the chair, because I'm yet again floored by how bad—in a good way—my wife is. I was going to fuck her face, but this invitation is too perfect to resist.

"You don't have to," I say comfortingly. "With me, you can be a slut."

She holds still, uncertain.

"Now turn around and lie over the table with your hands behind your back." We both love her vulnerability in this position.

She's shuddering with desire as she does as I tell her, pressing her tits flat to the pitch-black wood and linking her fingers at the small of her back.

With one deceptively casual movement, I flip her skirt up to reveal her arse and pretty cunt. Entirely naked. The scent of her arousal fills the air between us, and my mouth waters. I still love to eat her out. My favourite snack. Her pussy is pink, glistening, and as perfect as a rose. Thrusting into her is heaven, and the anticipation coils in me.

"Like this, Sir?" she says when I don't fall on her immediately, admiring her from a distance.

"Yes, good girl."

She purrs, and relaxes at my praise.

But she's only just able to look over her shoulder as I stand and position myself behind her.

"Spread," I command, and kick her feet further apart before she can move. "Open your legs wide, and take it like a good girl."

I angle my cock, and the second the crown touches where she's wet and yielding I ram all the way in.

She makes a shocked sound—real this time—of pain and pleasure. I'm big, so she tells me there's a pinch of discomfort on first entry.

She's tight. So tight. And with this little scene of hers, she's given me permission to use her, so I grasp her hips and pound into her, brutal and unforgiving. Maisie wouldn't come into my office on a day without the kids with no knickers on unless she wanted sex, as quick and filthy as possible.

The sight of her, so lewd, and of my cock disappearing into the slick heat of her pussy, is already threatening my control. I don't hold back. I let it happen, taking her as hard and deep as I need.

I can't get out words now, not to tell her how amazing she feels or that I love her more than anything. I can't even groan. My face must be savage, and I'm close, relishing my wife's submission. There are obscene sounds of the banging of my hips to her arse, my balls slapping onto her clit, and the juicy slide of me into her.

My balls are pulling up, and I'm ready to explode.

Then the phone rings.

Maisie twists to catch my eye and when I don't stop, ignoring it, her expression goes smug.

I am a fool for her, and she knows it, even when I have her helpless and impaled on my cock.

It takes a supreme effort to not come.

It's practically an act of god when I lean over, and snatch up my phone.

"Be a good, quiet girl for me," I tell her as she begins to whimper, seeing what I'm about to do. The words are as heavy a struggle as the massive weights I was lifting in the gym yesterday. "If you can be silent, I'll continue, and let you come."

"Sev, you arsehole," she hisses, and I grin.

Even so, my hand shakes as I answer the phone to my brother Rafe.

"Yeah," I say, and I'm impressed I sound pretty normal.

"Sev, there's a problem with..."

I pretend to listen. I pretend for Maisie, because I love that her cheeks heat as I hold her hands at the small of her back and glide oh-so-slowly in and out of her tight pussy. And I pretend for Rafe, making suitable noises of assent as he rants.

But I keep fucking her. Not as hard as before, and as the conversation continues, I release her hands and reach around her thigh to her clit.

"Are you listening, Sev?" Rafe demands.

"Not even slightly." All my attention is on my wife's clit, the side of her face where she's silently sobbing, and the way she's clenching on my cock, daring me to tip over. Luring me.

Then dragging me down.

I can't…

"You prick, this is important," Rafe snarls.

"Later." I get that one word out and manage to hang up, clumsily pressing with my thumb, before I wedge myself as deep into Maisie as I possibly can, once, twice, then stay there—in heaven, in my wife—right up against her cervix as I come in waves that wrack through me. White light, pleasure so intense it's almost pain. It's a whole body and mind workout to have sex with Maisie. My heart. Every muscle. My very soul fucks off to join her, probably leaving through the tip of my cock along with all my common sense, survival instincts, all my energy, and—obviously—the entire contents of my balls.

I'm silent, but my god it costs me. I'm a disaster. A wreck.

I drop the phone onto the floor and, hooking Maisie's waist, fall backwards onto my leather office chair, pulling her with me to lie on my lap. She comes, floppy and exhausted from being thoroughly fucked and from her orgasm. Looping her arms around my neck, she nestles into my chest. I hold her to me, and as my breathing gradually returns to normal, the familiar sense of peace descends.

Violence and control used to make me feel a bit like this, then sometimes I'd get a shadow of it, the merest outline of relief when I stalked Maisie. When I watched her. But now the only thing that makes me happy and at peace is my wife and my kids. In different ways, they make me whole.

I drop a kiss onto the top of Maisie's head, and I inhale the scent of my wife. Raspberries and cream.

"Think you can keep your job, sweetheart."

She shakes with laughter and nuzzles her face into my neck, biting me not-so-gently, and I give a growling purr. The smile on my face isn't unfamiliar anymore. But I tighten my grip on Maisie all the same.

*Mine.*

## THANKS

Thank you for reading, I hope you enjoyed it.

Want to read a little more Happily Ever After? Click to get exclusive epilogues and free stories! or head to EvieRoseAuthor.com

If you have a moment, I'd really appreciate a review wherever you like to talk about books. Reviews, however brief, help readers find stories they'll love.

Love to get the news first? Follow me on your favored social media platform - I love to chat to readers and you get all the latest gossip.

If the newsletter is too much like commitment, I recommend following me on BookBub, where you'll just get new release notifications and deals.

- amazon.com/author/evierose
- bookbub.com/authors/evie-rose
- instagram.com/evieroseauthor
- tiktok.com/@EvieRoseAuthor

Printed in Dunstable, United Kingdom